Wynn started with the muscles in Elsa's neck and shoulders, the healthy fingers of her left hand slowly working their way down Elsa's back and arms to her palms which didn't ache. Using her bad hand, she caressed Elsa's back in broad, circular strokes, lightly kneading her smooth skin. "This is a good workout for my fingers," she said.

They fell silent for a moment, Wynn soothing Elsa's battered body.

"Did you learn your lesson?" Wynn was concentrating on loosening an excruciating knot located in the middle of Elsa's right shoulder blade.

"Bronco riding's fast money if you win," Elsa replied. She luxuriated in her first ever body-rub. "Mm, that feels good."

"I'm an expert. I've given lots of rubdowns." Wynn moved downward to Elsa's buttocks...

Wynn worked toward Elsa's inner thigh area. The chafing from Papa's pants was no longer noticeable. An unusual heat gathered around Elsa's waist and just a little below that. The warmth wasn't like heat from the kitchen stove or the summer sun. It was more...penetrating. "I've never had a rubdown before. Those horses sure are lucky devils."

"You've decided you like it?"

"I've decided to become a horse. They get rubdowns more often than I ever will."

"I could give you one when you come visit next time."

Works by Penny Hayes

The Long Trail
Yellowthroat
Montana Feathers
Grassy Flats
Kathleen O'Donald
Now and Then

Now and Then

BY PENNY HAYES

THE NAIAD PRESS, INC.
1997

Printed in the United States of America on acid-free paper
First Edition
First Printing July, 1996
Second Printing February, 1997

Editor: Christine Cassidy
Cover designer: Bonnie Liss (Phoenix Graphics)
Typesetter: Sandi Stancil

Library of Congress Cataloging-in-Publication Data

Hayes, Penny, 1940 –
    Now and then / by Penny Hayes.
        p.   cm.
    ISBN 1-56280-121-X
    I. Title.
PS3558.A835N68   1996
813'.54—dc20

96-8546
CIP

To Brenda Teetsel
Eternal friend, extraordinaire

About the Author

Penny Hayes was born in Johnson City, New York, on February 10, 1940. As a child she lived on a farm near Binghamton, New York. She later went to school in Utica and Buffalo, graduating with degrees in art and special education. She has made her living teaching most of her adult life in both West Virginia and New York State.

She resides in Ithaca, New York. Her interests include backpacking, mountain climbing, canoeing, traveling, reading, and early American history. She has been published in *I Know You Know*, *Of the Summits Of the Forests* and various backpacking magazines. *Now and Then* is her sixth novel and she is working on her seventh.

This story is a work of fiction with freedoms taken in merging together both the fledgling Wild West shows and early rodeos. I have also taken some liberty with dates, but they are in close proximity to times during which these events took shape. No intent to discredit any real persons, living or dead, was planned.

Penny Hayes

CHAPTER ONE

In the year of 1888 and the month of July, Elsa Catulie was nearly eighteen years old. Although very shy, she was as obedient and gentle as parents could wish for in a daughter.

Her pale skin and long, drawn face lent her an aura of faint-heartedness. Had she any weight to her five-feet, eight-inch frame, and had she been blessed with breasts at least large enough to give her body some semblance of form, she might have been considered handsomely built. The only assets she felt she bore were her deep blue eyes and long lashes, thin, arching eyebrows and sculpted, narrow nose and lips. She also had a splendid tooth structure inherited from her mother and still beautiful because of a significant lack of confectioneries in her life. Most of the time she wore her black hair in a braid folded and pinned to the back of her head. Once in a while she wound it into a tight bun at the nape. Now and then she would bravely place a field flower, picked from along the sidewalk, in the flawless tress.

Elsa's dresses were plain blacks, browns or dark blues with just a sprinkle of white trim at the collar and cuffs. Her clothing was deliberately subdued in design to deter interested glances from others. She kept her eyes downcast whenever she left the house and often within the confines of her own home onn West Front Street in the town of Arrochar on Staten Island, where she and her parents lived.

In her two and a half years' of employment at Flowers' Department Store, she had never been late or absent. She spent a major portion of her life making an effort to offend no one.

She was painfully aware how different she was from other young women her age, unable to carry on small talk or giggle over trifling things others often found frightfully amusing. She had little interest in clothing, male or female friends or, for that matter, herself.

Elsa loved her father very much. He was a tall, bearded, gentle man with light blue eyes, a ready smile and a clear understanding that laughter was as crucial to life as was breathing. For work, he dressed in flannel shirts and coveralls. On Sunday, he wore his only black suit.

Elsa counted on Papa to lift her spirits at the end

of each day. He encouraged her to sing in the church choir or take long walks alone and didn't nag at her when she didn't do either. That was before Papa got her that job in East Arrochar as a favor somebody owed him, he said, and a job she took rather than endure the disappointed look on his face when she hesitated at hearing his tidings.

Elsa perceived Hellene, her tiny, plump, dark-eyed mother in an entirely different light. Years ago, Mama's braided hair had turned a dull, yellowish white. Decades of perpetual frowning had etched deep lines in her forehead and mouth, making her look closer to sixty than forty, which she had turned only last month. She was a stern disciplinarian who put work before family and nearly before God. She labored from the time she rose to when she flopped exhausted onto her bed at night. She seldom went anywhere except to confession on Saturday nights and to church on Sunday and holy days of obligation. She rarely dallied to gossip after Mass was over. She worked as hard as Papa did to help pay the bills. She seemed to have no other purpose in life.

Elsa seldom thought about Mama's sour feelings. It was just another rigid certainty in her life, something about which nothing could be done any more than one might single-handedly move a ten-ton boulder from one's path.

Elsa Catulie feared almost everything, particularly men. Men had the power to give and the power to take away. Men were akin to God and, like God, a puissant force to be reckoned with. She first experienced this hard fact at the young age of five when three men moved her parents, their furniture and her from their rented, tiny fifth-floor apartment

3

and out onto the street. Dozens of people gathered to cluck their tongues in sympathy and murmur words of consolation as the latest tenant was evicted by one of the ever-absent landlords on Arrochar's lower west side.

Clinging frantically to her mother's skirt, Elsa watched round-eyed and frightened as yet another piece of her life was carried through the door and unceremoniously plopped down beside Papa. This time it was her own little bed. Papa watched the movers' every action, bellowing and cursing at them if they were too rough with his possessions.

Mama knelt beside her and held her closely. "Papa needs to pay some money to someone more than he needs to pay the rent this month. But don't you worry, Elsa, honey. We'll be fine. Papa will see to it."

Elsa looked up at the opened windows of her home. Even the curtains that billowed in gentle breezes were gone. Effortlessly, the men had torn her life apart.

At first Elsa believed things would be all right just because Mama said so. But then the same thing happened again when she was nine and then, eleven.

The day she turned twelve years old, Elsa watched a brand new davenport, purchased in honor of her birthday, arrive and leave on the same day due to an unexpected debt Papa had to settle right away. Two men lifted the davenport that looked so pretty in the parlor as though it weighed nothing and loaded it onto the back of a waiting wagon. They drove off without a backward glance at the bitterly crying woman standing in the road, a wailing young girl beside her, and the man who was trying to console his weeping loved ones.

Earlier in the day, the same men had also been the ones who had delivered the davenport. Elsa thought, men gave, but more often than not, they took away.

Recently, Papa had purchased a fine bay horse with a star on his forehead and a buggy with black leather seats. Mama was so angry with him that she made him sleep in the living room for three nights before he was allowed back into his own bed. Papa drove his company's bread wagon; Mama didn't believe in owning a rig when everything her family might need could be achieved by a good, healthy walk to the store. She hated Papa's purchase even worse when Elsa began riding the horse and talking about it so much.

Elsa frequently rode the fourteen-hands-high gelding, each time feeling as though she had been reborn. The horse was the one thing in her life she completely trusted, even though she should have been afraid of the animal's huge size and his obnoxious skittishness with his new, inexperienced rider.

Confidently Elsa sat high in the air looking down on Papa's broad, proud, smiling face. He ran stubby fingers through his thick graying hair while giving her suggestions on how to sit sidesaddle.

On horseback, Elsa became whole. She was a complete being without doubt or fear racing the animal as fast as she could, learning to jump him over stone fences out of sight of the house, letting the wind yank the hat from her head and the pins from her hair. She was the one in control. On horseback, she felt a kindred spirit to Hurricane Nell, Mountain Kate, Bess the Trapper and others about whom she avidly read. They were the dauntless women of western fiction depicted in ten-cent novels and in monthly magazines, published at the slow, agonizing pace of one chapter per month. With a craving so powerful as to be almost painful, Elsa wanted to ride with these women. She longed to duplicate their lives, to live bravely as they did while facing terrible odds. She, like they, would cleverly use her keen intelligence, sharp wits and excellent handiwork with a gun to invariably save the day. Be it rustlers, robbers, kidnappers or debauchees of her fellow sisters, no situation would be too perilous no undertaking too difficult. Right would prevail; wrong would always be punished.

Since none of this was plausible or possible, and since the horse and buggy — much to Mama's relief and Elsa's devastating but private heartbreak — were lately sold to pay another of Papa's oppressive debts (the mortgage, food, household expenses) as he fought to improve his family's life, she contented herself with dreaming, reading dime novels and impatiently waiting for this year's arrival of the Wild West show.

Wild West shows, a combination of cowboy skills and fancy riding and shooting, were becoming popular in the East, with stops in the bustling cities of Chicago, Buffalo, Pittsburgh, New York and even as far away as England. Dazzling exhibitions were put together by enterprising men who recognized that the great buffalo hunt was finished, the Indian was no longer a major threat to western travelers and the mountain men were nearly extinct.

Bill Cody, Jack Garenger, Deck Blackhorn and other entrepreneurs who brought varying degrees of success and failure to these ventures began their exhibitions with flamboyant parades. This year, Wild Bill Cody's show arrived at Staten Island on a snow-white, twenty-six-car, special train. In the large, oval-shaped arena, there were scores of cowgirls and cowboys riding in formation carrying multicolored flags as well as that of the United States. Silver trim on horses' bridles and saddles brightly glittered. Guns loaded with blanks split the air with loud noises that made adults jump, children shout with glee and babies scream with fright. The parading people waved continuously at the invariably packed stands of cheering crowds surrounding them.

Performers wore broad-brimmed ten-gallon hats of white, tan, black, red or blue. Plaids, solid reds, oranges, blues, browns, blacks or yellow shirts and blouses were common. Pockets and yokes were trimmed with silver lacing, conches or fringe. Some of the men and women wore the more heavily fringed leather vests. Matching neckerchiefs were tied neatly around tanned throats. Cowboys wore black or brown pants of cloth or doeskin beneath leather chaps of tan, black or chalk white. Cowgirls wore equally fancy shirts womanly in cut and of a lighter weight material.

Considered quite daring for Eastern women's attire, the cowgirl's unique riding skirt was dyed either tan, chalk white, light blue, black or brown. The skirt was full, the hem heavily fringed, and was actually a pair of pants designed with two large leg openings. When standing, the cowgirl appeared to be dressed in a regular skirt, although it was just a bit

7

on the short side, exposing booted ankles. On horseback, the skirt allowed the ladies to comfortably straddle the horse.

Each show continued for three solid hours. Performers executed dazzling roping and shooting skills. Mounted cowboys chased after running calves. Lariats twirled in large circles over the men's heads were then let loose to flawlessly encircle the terrified calves' necks. The cowboys abruptly stopped their horses, flew from the saddle and ran to the animals. The confused calves halted midair at the end of the short ropes, landing hard against the earth and facing the opposite direction from which they had been headed. Sometimes before Elsa could count to five, three of the calf's legs were tightly bound together, the cowboys then leaping to their feet, their arms extending high into the air.

Cowboys rode saddled broncos and brahma bulls with only a rope secured around the bull's thick middle for a handhold. Some men were literally catapulted from the maddened animals' backs as though the riders had sprouted wings. They struck the ground with such force that it was a miracle they were able to stand and walk away. Hilarious clowns wearing painted faces and colorful, outrageous costumes distracted the crazed horses and bulls while their former riders painfully limped back to the starter chutes.

Riding against the clock and in figure eight formations, cowgirls raced swift steeds around heavy oak barrels painted orange. The horses ran at dangerous angles as their feminine riders urged them to even greater and more reckless speeds. The ladies also performed fancy roping and heart-stopping saddle tricks from the backs of galloping horses.

Not more than five feet tall, Annie Oakley, Little Sure Shot, with dark wavy hair and a youthful and lovely face sent shivers racing up Elsa's spine. With her magnificent shooting abilities, Oakley reduced thousands of spectators to silence by shattering a glass ball whirled on a string by her husband while sighting into a mirror and shooting backward over her shoulder. She wore a gray cowboy hat and a blue dress with a high white collar. The front of her bosom was covered with shooting medals she had won in past years. Elsa gawked.

Between reading ladies' western adventures, Ned Buntline's hundreds written about Buffalo Bill, and attending a Wild West Show with Papa this evening, Elsa Catulie was beside herself with joy.

Mama was on a rampage. "This is a waste of money and your time," she said sharply to them both. Prominent creases sliced her forehead and down both sides of her mouth.

"Oh, Mama," Papa said jovially. "One night out a year isn't going to hurt Elsa. I'll keep her close by my side all night." His eyes twinkled as he gave his wife's cheek an affectionate pinch.

Frowning darkly, Mama drew away. "It better not be all night. It better not be any longer than that terrible show is long."

Mama held a deep-seated distrust of show people. People who displayed themselves instead of doing an honest day's work infuriated her. Her mother hadn't raised her that way and her father tolerated no foolishness in their lives. "Your grandparents paid

9

dearly to come here and make a better life than they
had in Italy, and not work so hard. Well, they made
a better life, but the work is just as hard. Maybe
harder." Sweat poured down her face and soaked the
armpits of her dress. More angry yet, she said.
"Making money showing off. It ought to be against
the law. They should put all that money in St.
John's Poor Box where it'd do some good." She bent
over the kitchen's ever present ironing board. "This,"
she said, hefting a two-pound iron and pointing its
tip toward a shirt she was ironing, "is work. *Real*
work. Those show people don't work."

She allowed her enmity for her family's evening
outing to be so crystalline, so palatable that Elsa was
ready to back down, to not go, to endure crushing
disappointment rather than to suffer Mama's wrath.
She opened her mouth to tell Mama she'd changed
her mind and to apologize for being so thoughtless.
Papa glanced at her and put a quick hand on her
arm. His touch gave her strength to close her mouth.

Mama bent back to her task, muttering, "You
two'd best be in that Confessional come Saturday
night. Dreamers, the both of you." She banged the
iron onto the stove for reheating, yanked out its
portable handle, shoved it into the top of a second of
four more warming and waiting, and hefted the heavy
cast iron burden. With her back to them, she
announced, "I have nothing more to say."

CHAPTER TWO

Papa and Elsa left without another word to Mama. "It's true the show's only make-believe, Elsa," Papa said as they stepped off the front porch.

Plain though her black dress and black bonnet were, she wanted to look perfect for all the cowboys and cowgirls. She had even added a bit of Queen Anne's lace picked from alongside their house and stuck in her bonnet.

"I know it doesn't seem like work to Mama," Papa continued. "Those people look like they're having fun. But they work just as hard as Mama does. She just doesn't see it that way. As for you and me, and Mama too, should she give herself a rest now and then, we all need a change once in a while."

Elsa asked, "What do you do that's different, Papa, other than taking me to the Wild West shows?" Papa was as steady as a rock on his job, delivering bread six days a week and coming home at the same time every night.

"Little enough," he answered. "Little enough. But a man's got to have some small amusement in life or he dries up like an old clump of horse manure. I choose to see life as a game. That's my diversion."

"Not much of one, Papa." Elsa studied the hard-packed dirt and dung over which she and Papa walked. "Will we get there in time?" Papa had enough money for their tickets, but even at a nickel per person the cost of an omnibus was out of the question. With a seven-mile round-trip to the arena, she'd be dead tired by the time she got home tonight. Work would be dreadful tomorrow.

"If we hurry right along," Papa answered increasing his pace. Elsa hustled to keep up.

They arrived just as the parade began, having to content themselves with sitting in the upper grandstand. Ten thousand spectators were at this final night's presentation. They packed the bleachers from ground to top seat beneath the saltbox-shaped roof. Cody had brought along his own electric lights, still a marvel to Elsa, who remembered some man named Edison having invented lightbulbs in 1879. There would be little trouble seeing the show tonight. Vendors wove through the crowd, yelling, "Popcorn! Peanuts!"

"This looks grander than the show we saw two

12

years ago, Papa," Elsa said breathlessly. "They have a lot more events."

Her eyes quickly scanned many riders still moving in a great circle as their horses trotted sharply by and their flags smartly snapped. A small stagecoach drawn by a four-horse team rumbled by. The driver and guard yelled, "Hyah, hyah," adding further commotion to the excitement. Within the coach, well-dressed men in sleek dark suits and women in colorful, billowing gowns waved to the crowd through opened windows. Now and then the man riding shotgun fired blanks from his weapon, making the crowd jump from the sharp blast. Clowns paraded by on foot, causing hysterics among the children packed like soda crackers on front-row benches.

Elsa watched the entire event, her mouth hanging open. She marveled at the riders, the crazy horses and bulls and silly clowns. Later tonight she would lie in bed and recall every last detail she could. She would easily remember one of the female trick riders. Over the cheering spectators, she shouted, "That's Wynn Carson. She was here last time, Papa. I wish I could meet her."

It was a brave statement for Elsa. Meeting new people made her break out in a cold sweat. But then those people didn't ride upside down on a trotting horse. Those people made small talk, and lived lives as dull as her own. Those people knew nothing about her.

"We're to go straight home, Elsa. Mama's orders." He leaned toward her as he spoke, his arm touching hers. She liked the protective feeling he gave her. She was never afraid when he was near.

"I wouldn't take long, and I'd walk especially fast

going home to make up the time." She felt pitiful. Her voice sounded pitiful even to her own ears. "Please, Papa." She sounded like a child and she knew it.

At the conclusion of the show, Papa said nothing about meeting the trick rider as they slowly made their way down to the grounds. In the luminous electric lights, dust swirled in the air, riled by hundreds of animals and thousands of people sluggishly moving toward several exits surrounding the arena.

Papa chewed his lower lip, his thick moustache riding up and down beneath his nose. Elsa's stomach churned while she silently prayed he hadn't forgotten her request.

They moved slowly, drawing closer and closer to the exit. With each step Elsa's hopes dwindled a little more.

Papa grabbed her elbow. "All right. We can't get out right now, anyway."

Elsa's relief was so immense that only the compact crowd kept her suddenly weakened knees from buckling beneath her.

"This way," Papa said. They fought their way to the left ultimately passing through the thinning population. At the show's campgrounds, he asked a tired-looking cowboy where Wynn Carson might be found.

The lanky man removed his hat and spoke with a soft Texas drawl. "Stables. Over there and to your left."

Papa quickly thanked him. "Come on, honey. We'll have to hurry."

14

Elsa swallowed with anticipation and coughed up fine dust billowing like fog in the air.

They soon found the stables and Wynn Carson. "There she is, honey. Go on, say hello."

Papa remained behind as Elsa nervously walked toward the fancy saddle rider. Still dressed in a white skirt and blouse, Wynn was brushing her beautiful horse's blond coat. The large animal was damp with sweat. Wynn threw a blanket over his back and rump. "There, boy," she said. "You won't get chilled." She saw Elsa approaching. "Hello," she said. Her smile calmed Elsa, but only a little.

Elsa cleared her throat and stammered her name. "I'm . . . I'm Elsa Catulie." She collected her wits as Wynn again smiled at her.

Wynn Carson was as tall as Elsa, her hazel eyes looking directly into Elsa's. Her light brown hair was pulled back in a single braid, revealing flawless, tanned skin. Her eyes had a merriment about them as though she might break out into laughter at any second. Her lips were full and her teeth white and straight. She was what many men would call a handsome woman. She carried herself with unquestionable confidence and pride.

When she spoke, Elsa was surprised at the deep tenor of her voice. "It's nice to meet you," she said. "I'm Wynn Carson and this is Buttons, the famous palomino." Wynn reached up and scratched behind Buttons' ear. "And dearly loved."

"I can see that." Elsa admired the big animal's smooth coat, his shimmering silver tail and mane, his clear eyes and quivering nostrils. "I watched you ride here in 'eighty-six in a different show."

The trick rider extended her hand. Her palm had the texture of well-seasoned, hardened leather. Her handshake crushed Elsa's. Elsa let go immediately. "We have a better show this year. Don't you think?"

Elsa nodded, saying, "It's nice to see you riding again. I like your new trick. It's very daring." Wynn's new trick was to hang off the side of the saddle with only a boot in one stirrup and one hand clinging to Buttons' tail, her free hand and foot held unfettered away from the horse while he trotted twice around the arena. She was one of only a handful of women who performed maneuvers from the saddle. "You'd have to be very strong for a trick like that."

Buttons snorted loudly. Elsa stumbled backward, thinking the horse was going to nip her.

"Stop it, Buttons," Wynn scolded, jerking his halter. "He's just showing off. That's his own trick when someone new is around."

Reassured, Elsa stepped forward again. "He certainly scared me." With a frankness that surprised her, she added, "But then, everything does." A faint smile passed across her face.

"You don't look like the timid type," Wynn said. Her words pleasantly shocked Elsa; that someone would believe that of her!

"I am," Elsa replied. "May I pet your horse?"

Wynn moved aside so that Elsa could stand beside Buttons. She ran her hand down his smooth neck feeling powerful muscles ripple as he lightly shook his head. "He's so beautiful." Elsa kept her hand pressed against him, absorbing his strength and beauty.

Papa approached them. "How do you do, Miss

Carson?" Gallantly, he bowed saying, "We enjoyed watching you ride." He then turned to Elsa. "It's time to go, honey."

Audaciously, spontaneously, Elsa blurted, "Would you care to write, Miss Carson? I'd answer every letter." Blood boiled loudly in her ears. Her face burned as though she were standing over a roaring cookstove.

"Now, honey," Papa said. "I'm sure Miss Carson is very busy, and Mama's waiting." He smiled at Wynn and began walking toward an exit.

Elsa gave a desperate glance at Wynn and then ran after him. She grabbed his coat, stopping him. "But, Papa, you *want* me to meet people," she whispered in quiet desperation. She was so scared of her uncommon brazenness she thought she might vomit. "You *said* so."

"Could you wait just a minute, please, sir?" Wynn called out. Without waiting for Papa's answer, she tossed aside her brush and disappeared into a nearby stall. She returned immediately with a small poster in her hand. Using Buttons' flank as a writing surface, she scribbled something on the back and rolled it up. Handing it to Elsa, she said, "I'd love to hear from you. And please call me Wynn."

Elsa nodded, unable to speak. She had seen the poster here and there around her neighborhood along with dozens of others advertising the coming show. On this poster, Wynn hung upside down from one side of the saddle, clinging to the horse only by one booted foot in a thong attached to the saddle horn and one hand thrust through a stirrup. Elsa clutched the prized poster to her breast. "I'll write soon," she said over her shoulder as she and Papa hurried away. "And if you're here next year, I'll come to see you ride again."

"Stop afterward, too," Wynn said. She smiled radiantly, and Elsa gave away her heart to the only person other than family who had ever directly asked her to visit.

She and Papa walked home even more swiftly than they had come. Elsa's legs ached, and Papa was limping a bit too. "This was a wonderful evening, Papa." She tucked her hand into his, clutching the poster with the other. It felt nice to be so cared about. Papa was busy it was true, up early, home late, but when he was home, he made her feel unique. "I'll never forget this evening, Papa. You've made it wonderful."

He squeezed her hand and nodded as they hustled along.

Nearly home, an unfamiliar carriage drew just ahead of them and stopped. The windows were concealed with darkened shades. A man dressed in a black suit and snow-white shirt jumped out and faced them. He stood straddle-legged and unmoving. His tall height and large belly reminded Elsa of an oak tree about to topple over.

With the street lantern burning behind him, Elsa couldn't clearly make out the man's features, but she did see her father's face, pale. "What is it, Papa?"

"A little misunderstanding earlier today, honey. I'll just have a talk with this fine gentleman, and we'll be on our way."

Elsa watched with fascinated horror as the stranger drew a small gun hidden inside his coat pocket. From seven feet away he pointed it directly at Papa's head. "You ain't ever gonna talk to anybody again, Blacky. You had your last chance today."

"Who's Blacky, Papa?" Elsa asked. Her father's name was John.

The gun went off blowing a hole between his two disbelieving eyes. He crumpled at Elsa's feet.

The well-dressed man took a step toward her. Inches from her face he warned, "You make one sound, and I'll shoot you too."

She was incapable of making any sound. She was incapable of moving as the deadly stranger retreated into his carriage and drove off as though nothing had happened.

She remained paralyzed for perhaps five minutes, only barely breathing before she could bring herself to look down upon the man who, just brief moments ago, had made her feel like a real person for a whole evening. Blood trickled from the hole in his forehead. Something warm slid down her cheek. She thought tears. She brushed them away feeling sand on her fingers. She studied the tiny particles. They were bloodied bits of bone fragment from Papa's skull.

Then she screamed.

CHAPTER THREE

The funeral was a three-day affair attended by relatives, neighbors, the police who questioned Elsa daily and admitted they'd probably never find the killer and a number of people who knew Papa from his bread route of the past several years. In hushed tones, folks spoke to Mama who had been weeping from the time she learned of Papa's death until the last pat of dirt on his grave covered him forever. Fleetingly, they touched Elsa's shoulder to say how sorry they were. She merely nodded, unable to speak, overcome by her own terrible loss.

Before the burial, when Papa was laid in the living room for two days, a few unknown men, expensively dressed and all strangers, came to the house. They visited at different hours both evenings. Each stopped by the casket and looked without emotion upon Papa's waxen face. Neither Elsa nor Mama knew them.

Sometimes one man and sometimes two would quietly approach Mama, who sat on a straight-backed chair between her husband's coffin and Elsa, who sat equally as rigid to her right. Mama clutched Elsa's hand throughout the long days, releasing her only when asked by the gentlemen to step into the kitchen for a private word or two. The first time Mama willingly followed. Obviously she had no idea what they were going to say to her. After that, any stranger wanting to speak alone with her caused her to tremble. Altogether, four different strangers talked to her.

"Who are they?" Elsa whispered. She could feel Mama's hand sweating in her own. By then she had absorbed her mother's intense fear. "What do they want?"

Mama never replied.

Elsa was glad when the grave was filled and she and Mama could walk away from the cemetery. The tension of it all had caused her stomach to cramp and rumble since yesterday. Now her remaining family could go home and figure out what to do next without worrying about some newcomer scaring Mama and, in turn, her, out of their wits.

They hung their wraps on the coat tree and migrated to the kitchen. "I'll make us some coffee," Mama said. Each with a fresh cup before them, they sat at the table. Mama spoke firmly. "Elsa, I want you to listen very carefully to me."

It greatly relieved Elsa to once again hear Mama's old familiar, strong voice. At least that much of her seemed to have returned. She'd barely spoken above a whisper, conspicuously sinking within herself and talking only in subdued tones from the time she'd learned Papa was dead to this moment.

"From now on, Elsa, you will give me your full wages."

"My wages? All of it?" Elsa was already handing over most of her salary, but she'd always kept back a little for her western novels and bolts of cotton.

"Every penny. We'll need all of it just to stay alive. Now with Papa gone . . ."

"All right, Mama, but . . ." Guilt lay like a heavy shroud upon Elsa's shoulders, and she cast her eyes to the floor as she said, "I'd like to keep a half-dollar each month."

"Not a cent!" Mama's eyes took on a strange, desperate look. Dark purple half-moons shaded the puffy flesh beneath them. She looked tired to the bone.

"What bills do we still have, Mama, other than the mortgage and house bills and the rest of Papa's funeral expenses?" A half-dollar a month wasn't much to ask for.

"Just let me handle the money. It'll be better if I do." Mama rose slowly, using her hands to laboriously push herself up and away from the table. She glowered ferociously as her lips drew into two thin, white lines beneath her large nose. Elsa watched her until she disappeared into her parents' bedroom. The latch quietly clicked as the door closed behind her.

Elsa remained at the table, slowly studying the familiar kitchen, place of hundreds of meals, quiet talks, Papa nearby scuffing his restless feet against the worn linoleum beneath the table. The wallpaper was old, faded and yet comforting. It was a small room for the amount of work Mama did here. A combination cook- and woodstove kept the kitchen warm during winter; a tiny broom closet was stuffed with empty canning jars, cloth rags, boots, a mop and broom; a few preserves were neatly stacked on a shelf.

She glanced into the living room. The davenport, a big, flowered, heavy affair, bought secondhand and threadbare after all these years, was comfortable to sit upon. A small table with a chimney lantern and a photograph of her parents taken years ago was placed nearby. Two equally worn overstuffed chairs were also part of the room. A big rag rug helped keep the floor warm during cold nights.

Papa and Mama's room contained two beds and a single dresser. Nails pounded into a far wall held any clothing requiring a hanger. A long time ago, Mama had made two small rugs, one for each side of their bed.

Elsa's own room was equally simple. The bed and small dresser were almost all that it contained. A mirror she picked up at a sale sat on the dresser and leaned against the wall. Her clothing also hung from nails. On the wall beside her bed she had tacked up the poster Miss Carson had given her portraying her doing a daredevil stunt, clinging from the saddlehorn and one stirrup with both feet. Buttons looked to be at a dead gallop. A crowd cheered from behind.

Near Elsa's room, a door harboring a narrow set of stairs led to an attic used for storage where there were a few items of clothing, a trunk or two and several empty boxes that hadn't been repacked since they had moved.

The house wasn't pretty. It needed paint and new wallpaper and more furniture, but it was theirs. There was a mortgage, but it was being paid regularly. When first moving in three years ago, Elsa had fallen in love with the place not for its beauty but because they owned it! Papa promised her the day they moved that no matter what, this house would always be her home and no one would take it from her. So far he had kept his promise. But now he was dead. Elsa wondered if the promise would hold.

She sighed. Her stomach had settled considerably since leaving the cemetery. There would be no more people wandering in and out of the house. A dead man would not be laid out in the living room. No longer would she anticipate seeing the coffin lid close over Papa's face hiding him from her forever or watch the casket slowly lowered into a hole in the ground.

She looked forward to going back to work. If it meant enduring a bit of cruelty from her boss, then that was infinitely more acceptable than the past several agonizing days of her life had been.

Resting her hands in her lap, she felt the black cotton dress pull against her skin. Closing her eyes, she pretended she could hear Mama and Papa talking in their room. They had always chatted about something, usually about some funny thing that had happened to Papa that day on his run and how Mama's day had gone, how much work she'd accomplished, how many shirts or dresses she'd ironed.

Elsa glanced at the chain watch hanging from her neck. Were Papa alive, he would just be coming home, late in the afternoon and hungry enough to eat his supper plate. Mama would miss him terribly, Elsa knew, his willingness to listen to her same old daily stories. She would miss hearing him dress up his stories like fancy gifts to make her laugh even more. Mama never laughed much, but she always did when Papa first got home, before being once again consumed by duty.

Elsa wandered into the living room and sat dispiritedly on the davenport. She reached for her parents' photograph and studied it closely for probably the hundredth time since Papa had been shot three days ago.

She thought about how Mama and he seemed to be one person most of the time and how clearly each loved the other. Still, Mama bitterly criticized his never bringing home enough money to get ahead, let alone break even. This was the only thing Elsa knew that bothered Mama about Papa. Mama's eyes lighted up till they sparkled like fireworks on the Fourth of July whenever Papa brought home some special item like a new davenport or a fancy chair. Mama's eyes blazed more like a fire raging out of control when the men hauled it off, usually not long after. Then Mama wouldn't speak to him for weeks while Elsa tiptoed around the house trying to appear invisible.

25

She gave up thoughts of cooking supper. Instead she went to bed and for the next seven hours waited for sleep to come.

Several blocks east of Elsa's house on Front Street near Arrochar proper, was Flowers' Department Store. Elsa worked in lingerie at the same low rate of pay at which she'd originally started, never having been offered a raise and never having dared ask for one.

Miss Marie Ashley was Elsa's immediate supervisor. Ashley was a harpy shrew, Elsa thought, overly burdened with a fondness for herself. Miss Ashley was stunningly beautiful and delicately built, her black hair worn in a swirl atop her head. Her exquisite face beamed with kindness toward everyone, it seemed, but Elsa, an inner glow radiating from her dark brown eyes and devastating smile. She was willowy, yet graceful as a swan. She dressed exclusively in garments sold by Flowers'.

Marie Ashley was kind and gracious to customers, yet Elsa hated her passionately. She had often made Elsa feel no better than the decaying horse droppings that lay rotting in the streets. At any time she could be expected to walk up to Elsa and out of earshot of other employees, quietly say, "Have you been bargain hunting again, dear? Hmmm?" She would carelessly flip her delicate hand toward Elsa's dress and give her that detestably winning smile that Elsa hated so much. At other times, Ashley would scold her for not having sold more lingerie or worked faster or harder. Unable to please her, Elsa had given up trying after two years' effort.

"She likes the others," Elsa would whisper to the trees lining her walk. "Why not me?"

Ashley tolerated timorous behavior in no woman; not since first meeting Marietta Stow four years ago.

In 1884, Marietta Stow, the first woman in the United States to be nominated for Vice President, spoke at a modest gathering of women in Burkley Hall, located three blocks south of Flowers'. Stow endorsed protection of suffrage, widows' rights and racial equality. Ashley never let anyone forget that stellar moment in her life when, following the lecture, Mrs. Stow walked up the aisle and shook Ashley's hand as women reached out to touch the modern thinker.

It was a story Ashley repeated to every new employee. "Such a brave woman. She is a woman to follow. I'd go to hell or to jail for her."

Ashley's disparaging treatment of Elsa had created a loathing of her job. Since the funeral, however, and for several months past, Elsa's attitude had slowly changed toward working in lingerie. It had everything to do with having personally met the marvelous Wynn Carson. Often while Elsa straightened shelves of delicate garments made of fine bobbin lace, she pretended she was selecting the costume Wynn would wear in her show that evening. She was Wynn's personal dressing maid, selecting only the best lingerie, well decorated with delicate hand stitches, smooth, shiny silk and some with enough whalebone in the corsets to keep a drunk from falling down.

Weekly, Elsa wrote to Wynn; eventually she took to wandering among the women's dresses during part of her lunch time, mentally choosing only the finest dresses from the racks, memorizing the color, design, texture and fit.

At night she lay in bed ignoring her prayers in

favor of the more thrilling and imaginative images she concocted behind closed lids. She imagined helping Wynn into the new wardrobe she had decided upon for that day. That the style of dress was completely impractical to wear while hanging upside down from a moving horse didn't occur to her. The searing red gown with pearl buttons centered from breast to waist would looking dashing against Buttons' golden coat, or the expensive deep blue velvet one with the wide sash and front line cut so low she'd have every man staring at her and every woman envying her. In these beautiful garments, she would help Wynn mount her great horse and afterward rush to the front stands and cheer until her throat was raw as Wynn daringly rode around and around the arena doing tricks that would kill an ordinary rider.

Elsa fretted that Wynn hadn't answered a single one of her letters. Each day when she came home from work, her disappointment was renewed at having received no mail and lingered until the following morning when she could hope all over again. And equally as worrisome, she had just used the last of her savings and sent her final letter to Miss Carson.

Within days, unable even to buy a single stamp from time to time to write more letters, Elsa slipped into a melancholy from which she could not recover. Although they'd only met once, and very briefly at that, yearning to see the show girl brought tears to Elsa's eyes. With Papa gone it would be impossible to see Wynn ever again.

Lately, Mama seemed in better shape than Elsa. Their financial troubles appeared to be under control beneath her iron hand. For tonight's supper, they munched on beans, squash and slices of bacon and bread while chatting about the tons of clothing Mama ironed today and the number of rich ladies Elsa had served. A hard knock at the door echoed throughout the house, shattering their thoughts.

Fear cascaded through Mama's eyes. "Now who could that be at suppertime who doesn't just walk in?" She was referring to either of her two sisters along with their several children.

Elsa rose. "Sit still, Mama. I'll get it."

"No!" Mama's sharp command seated Elsa instantly. She lowered her eyes to her plate and forked a piece of bacon she knew she wouldn't be able to swallow. Her hands quivered as her stomach knotted as tight as tangled hair.

Mama went into the living room. Elsa couldn't bear being left behind and followed, stopping at the kitchen doorway.

Mama opened the door. A large man in a dark brown business suit made his way inside before he could say, "Evening, ma'am." He seemed to fill the room as he kicked the door shut behind him with his highly polished black boot. With a flourish, he removed his hat, lessening his height not a whit. The skin of his face was severely pitted and his dark eyes were set deep in his skull. He towered over Mama like a gnarled old tree.

Backing away several feet, she asked, "Is there a problem?"

"Brought your mail, Mrs. Catulie," he said politely in a low, rumbling voice. Only his mouth grinned while his eyes remained cold and piercing. "Saw it in your street box."

"Thank you." Mama took the mail from him and tossed it onto the table next to the davenport. "What do you want?"

"You're keeping up. That's good. Come to remind you." The stranger stared openly at Elsa.

Mama stepped in front of him. "I'm keeping my word." Her eyes were fixed upon his face. "You have no business here."

Ignoring her comment, he scanned the house's interior. "Some place you got here. Not much furniture. Firetrap."

"You have no business here," Mama repeated firmly. "Please leave."

He did, saying as he turned, "Pretty daughter."

Mama opened the door and ever so gently closed it behind him. Elsa suspected Mama wanted to tear the door from its hinges and hurl it at the big man who was making his way off the porch.

"Who is he, Mama?" Timidly, she pulled back the curtain and glanced out the window. "He's leaving."

Mama sank on the nearest chair. "Thank God." She lowered her face to her hands and sat stone still for several minutes. Elsa remained paralyzed before her. Finally Mama said, "He's an old acquaintance of your Papa's." She snorted like an angry horse. "Best thing for me is to lay down for a while. You go ahead and finish eating without me. If I say anything else, God'll snatch me up right now because it won't be proper wording for a lady."

Elsa's pulse returned to normal as she heard Mama's door close. She idly picked up the mail. Being home all the time, Mama always saw it before anybody else. Even Papa. It was unusual that tonight she hadn't thought to bring it in before.

There was just one piece, a letter. A real letter! Such mail was rare in this household. She stared unbelieving at it. In fine script, *Elsa Catulie* was written on the front of the envelope. Several seconds passed before the return address fully sank in. Wynn Carson! According to the address, she was here, right here on Staten Island, and not too many blocks away. An omnibus could get Elsa there in no time.

With trembling hands and a renewed pounding of her heart she sat and opened the letter, the first ever from Wynn. Elsa had written so many times. Too many? Is that what prompted Wynn to write? Had Elsa become a pest? Was Wynn about to tell her to stop bothering her?

Tentatively she lifted the flap and pulled out a single sheet of paper. The penmanship was graceful and flowing. The world around her receded into oblivion as she read, "My dearest Elsa."

"Give me that." The letter and envelope disappeared so fast from Elsa's grasp that she hardly knew they were gone.

"Mama!" Elsa leaped to her feet. "That's *my* letter."

Wordlessly, Mama marched into the kitchen and lifted the stove lid. Elsa was tight on her heels. Embers still glowed from the fire used to cook the evening meal. Elsa watched as Mama thrust the letter into the firebox and it burst into flames. In seconds, Wynn's longed-for words disintegrated to ash.

Mama slammed down the lid with a crash. "I'll not have my daughter corresponding with show people." She yanked open a small closet door and pulled out the ironing board. From the stove's breadwarmer she drew out her irons. In seconds, she had stoked the firebox, the double-pointed irons lined up like unyielding soldiers on warming trivets. Mama tugged a blouse from the never-emptied basket of clothing, snapping it hard. *"This* is honest work."

She had said that the night Papa died. "Have there been other letters, Mama?" Elsa asked. "Did you take other letters from Wynn?"

"Yes! All of them." Mama picked up an iron and spit on its bottom. It barely sizzled. She slammed it down.

"Where are they?" Elsa placed her hands on the back of the chair, steadying herself. Her knuckles turned white beneath her grip.

"Gone."

For a moment, a blinding, black rage exploded behind Elsa's eyes as she visualized other letters from Wynn, the pages curling from the heat as the fire consumed them. How many others had she destroyed?

"Then give me money so that I can write to Wynn and tell her what's going on. She has a right to know."

"I'll give you nothing," Mama answered.

"One stamp, Mama! That's all I'm asking— *begging* — for. I can use scrap paper and make my own envelope."

"Go to bed. Now!" Mama's eyes froze upon Elsa's.

Her heart and courage shriveled in her breast as she left Mama to do her "honest" work. She would labor throughout the night just to prove her point.

One thing Mama didn't count on though. She remembered Wynn's address perfectly. *Perfectly!* On her next payday, she would demand money for the omnibus, and she would go to visit Wynn.

CHAPTER FOUR

The long winter had passed and with it its depressing and frugal holidays. A wet and rainy spring was upon them. Elsa likened her spirit to that of a rotting vegetable. Soon there would be nothing left to salvage even for the poorest of salads.

More weeks had slid by. Helplessly, Elsa had handed Mama her wages without asking for travel fare. But since Thursday, November sixteenth, at seven p.m., the time when Elsa watched while Mama destroyed Wynn's letter, not once had she given up the idea.

One Saturday evening while Elsa washed dishes, Mama retrieved the money jar from the broom closet. Almost reverently, she spread the coins and bills out on the table. Dollar by dollar, coin by coin, she separated the scanty resources into a few small stacks. "Groceries," she muttered. "Church. Extra." The "extra" pile contained the bulk of the cash.

Elsa looked over her shoulder. "A lot of money for that pile, Mama, and not much to show for it."

"You know how it goes, Elsa."

Elsa didn't know how it went, or why. Mama began putting the money into different envelopes and humming a tuneless song. Maybe it was a good time to ask for travel fare, Elsa thought. There seemed to be no reason why she couldn't see Wynn this evening. She became giddy with pleasure. She and Wynn would discuss horses, costumes, tricks and show people. She would ask Wynn about every place she'd ever performed. She'd ask if Wynn had ever been afraid of falling off Buttons. If Wynn could stand it, Elsa would talk with her all night long. "I was thinking, Mama, about visiting Wynn Carson this evening."

"Nonsense." Mama's face set like concrete. The pupils of her eyes became tiny black pinpoints fastening themselves upon Elsa's. "You don't need to be messing with show people. They're tramps. Every damn one of them." She stood and stepped close to Elsa, Elsa feeling as though she were being dwarfed by Mama.

Elsa cracked. Soap and water slopped all over the back wall and onto the floor as she gave the rag a mighty heave into the dishpan.

Mama raised her hand to slap Elsa's face.

Stunned by her fury, Elsa still managed to grasp her wrist. "Don't you dare hit me." They froze glaring at each other. Elsa released her.

Mama hissed, "I will not allow you to see her. Ever. She's show business."

Silently Elsa left, going to her room, fighting the urge to run away from this place, from this awful confining life.

She sat on the bed and looked at Wynn's poster, then closed her eyes. In the room's semi-darkness every detail of the poster was indelibly etched upon her mind. She could close her eyes and see it, its image so strong she needn't bother looking at it. "I'd come if I could, Wynn," she whispered. "We'd visit and have a grand time." If only she'd been allowed to keep at least one of Wynn's letters . . .

Taking along a lantern, she fled to the attic in a devouring gulf of despair. With only a small four-pane window on the west end to cast muted light and blurred shadows, it was there that she often retreated with a book or a thought.

She sat down on an old beat-up traveling trunk by the window. The trunk had been Papa's, full of old junk, he'd said. From time to time she wondered why he had always kept it locked. Not even Mama opened it. But it made a fine seat upon which to sit and stare out the window and dream dreams, most of them lately centering upon Wynn and how close by she was. If only Elsa could muster up enough courage to ask for omnibus fare.

Rain began to fall, adding to her awful gloom. It was mid-May, and not even today's weather was agreeable.

She struggled to understand her mother's

thinking. "Why, Mama, why? Wynn's a good person. She likes me." She rocked back and forth, pounding her fists against her thighs. In rhythm with the increasing downpour, her steady thrashing of herself and her question echoing in her mind, she whispered over and over, "Why, why, why?"

She leaped up and released her terrible anger with a vicious kick to the old trunk. A flurry of additional blows caused one side to cave in and then another and finally the lid burst open, attached only by a single, twisted metal hinge.

Dazed, she stared at the carnage.

Why, there was really nothing in the thing, just an old book of some kind and a brown envelope. Elsa collected its scant contents and sat amongst the wreckage of leather and wood. The book was a ledger listing several men's names she had never heard Papa mention. Beside each name were dates and dollar amounts reaching back to long before she was born.

Its contents meaningless, she set aside the journal and opened the envelope. She withdrew a tattered old photograph once ripped into several fragments, then carefully reassembled and pasted onto a small piece of cardboard. She slanted the picture toward the light, examining its images. "Mama and Papa," she whispered.

Papa was holding the reins of a sleek, beautiful black horse. Beside him stood Mama. An inner light seemed to shine from Papa's face. Mama looked very beautiful.

Elsa studied her parents and the fine horse. As far back as she could remember she had never seen Papa beaming quite like he was in this picture, looking as though he owned the world. Mama didn't look much different than she did today except that she was younger and thinner. There was also a distinct sadness about her face.

Elsa examined the background closely. Behind Papa and Mama were stables. There was a sign over one of the doors. She squinted as she read, "Race Track."

A sick feeling crept into her stomach as she put aside the photograph and again picked up the ledger. She looked more carefully this time, starting with the most recent entry. Papa had owed someone money the night he was shot. She flipped the pages backward looking for the same man's name. There it was again. But Papa still owed him money. She searched for another entry finding several more for numerous names that were duplicated and shown to have received money from Papa, yet still he owed them more. He never seemed to catch up.

It wasn't possible, she thought. She wished the trunk was in one piece again with its strong lock holding her world together. But that time had passed. She had no choice but to move on, forever, until death.

Elsa gathered the ledger and photograph and moved sluggishly toward the door. The trunk, completely destroyed, looked like what it truly was: a repository of years and years of lies.

"Papa," she whispered. "Why did you do this to me, to Mama?"

She went downstairs to face her new life.

CHAPTER FIVE

Mama sat at the table, a cup of coffee in her trembling hands, and tears filling her eyes. Elsa flung the book and photo on the table, barely able to keep from throwing it in Mama's face. Mama fixed her eyes upon the objects, saying nothing, tears coursing down her round cheeks.

"Papa lied to me all my life, Mama. You lied by covering up for him. He gambled away every penny he ever made, didn't he?" Mama made no move to answer. Elsa braced her hands on the table and leaned into Mama's face. *"Didn't he?"*

Speaking barely above a whisper, Mama said, "He was your father."

"He was a lying thief, and to this day he steals from us both. Who's Blacky?"

"Blacky?" Mama rose slowly and moved behind her chair, positioning her hands firmly on its back.

"The man called Papa Blacky just before he shot him."

Mama lowered her head, not looking at Elsa. "It was a nickname given to him after a big race his horse had won. The horse's name was Blacky. Once in a while, Papa was called that. It was a sort of good luck name for him."

Elsa's eyes were wet with accusatory anger. "And now you and me have to pay up some kind of a debt, don't we? That's what all that whispering was at the funeral. Those fancy men wanting you to pay it — and me. I didn't even know Papa did such things. He seemed so . . . so perfect." She collapsed in a chair and wept bitterly, her head in her arms.

Mama came around and put her hand on Elsa's shoulder. "If we don't, honey, they're gonna kill you and me. They said they'd burn down the house, too. It's the only thing Papa ever managed to hang onto. And it wasn't easy for him."

"But I didn't cause this, Mama," Elsa screamed. "We're penniless, completely penniless."

"We'll be homeless and dead if we don't keep paying them something each week, child." Her voice was shaking but level.

Elsa swept Mama's consoling hand from her shoulder. "How much do we owe, Mama? How much does *Papa* owe, because *I* don't owe anybody anything."

Mama again touched Elsa, this time squeezing her daughter's bony shoulder until Elsa winced. "You do owe, child, because Papa's dead, and he can't do anymore. You owe because he never let you go hungry, and you never went naked. Papa bought this house and fought like a crazy man to hang onto it." Mama moved close to Elsa's face. "Papa had an affliction . . ."

"He was a lying gambler, Mama. He gambled away money that could have made our lives a whole lot easier."

This time Mama succeeded in cracking her daughter across her face. Bright, white dots danced before Elsa's eyes. Mama's cold voice said, "Your ingratitude sickens me. Your papa was my husband, and I'll not have anyone speaking that way about him. Yes," she conceded, "he lied, and he gambled, but he did it because he couldn't help himself. More than once I could have shot him myself, he made me so mad. But he came home every night, and I slept in his arms. Not a lot of women can say that about their husbands."

Shocked that Mama hit her, Elsa put her hand to her burning cheek. In her rage, she would like to have challenged that declaration, too. Acidly, she said, "You loved him too much."

"Yes, I did. That was my only mistake where he was concerned."

Hopelessness overcame Elsa. "How much do we owe, Mama?" She didn't want the house burned down, and she didn't want Mama or herself killed.

"Eight thousand dollars."

Elsa picked up the ledger. "Mama, look at this final entry. It's only a thousand dollars."

"That may be, Elsa, but four different men came to me with figures that added up to eight thousand dollars. I have no way to prove Papa didn't owe that much. So we'll pay."

"But the ledger." Elsa extended it toward Mama.

Mama's face became red with large blotchy spots on her neck and cheeks. She threw herself into the chair opposite Elsa, her hands outspread. "What do you want me to do, Elsa? Go to the police? What could I tell them? That Papa is being cheated by bad men even though he's dead, and even though he himself was a gambler? They'd laugh me right out of the station. Maybe even put me in jail because I knew about it and never told them. The law isn't kind, Elsa. Not one damn bit."

"Then let's get a lawyer."

"With what? We have pennies left after each accounting to these leeches. Elsa, you're Papa's poor daughter, and you'll help clear his debt. It won't last forever. Maybe twenty years."

Elsa's body went rigid, her fists clenched in her lap. "Fine. I'll be an old woman by then with no chance to earn any money for myself." One day she had hoped to marry and have her own life. "My father did this to us, to me. My lying, deceiving father has taken it all away. Bit by bit, piece by piece, year after year. His deceit . . ." She couldn't control herself. "Liar, liar, liar," she raved, childlike. "Thief, thief, thief."

Mama came around the table and towered over Elsa. Elsa recoiled, anticipating another vicious slap. Mama roared and spittle flew from her mouth. "I can't listen to this rubbish anymore. I won't." She moved back a step, her hands balled at her sides.

"You make me sick with your ridiculous, oh-so-delicate ways." She stalked from the kitchen, a wrathful string of curses trailing behind her as she damned every man who had ever walked the earth. Her bedroom door rattled the dishes in the cupboards as she slammed it shut.

Elsa shook her head to clear it. How, she wondered, had Mama ever borne up under such a terrible burden for so many, many years? Elsa doubted that she understood one single thing about either of her parents.

Cumbersome, tall walls built of weighty bricks of depression fell in on her. She could barely make her way to her room after this horrifying discovery.

She sank to the bed, thinking: years to pay. Years and years.

Seconds later, Mama appeared at her door. "I don't want you turning out like your Papa, Elsa. That's the only reason I don't want you near anybody who works with horses. I've met dozens of people, both men and women, who destroy themselves in their belief that they can beat the odds. It never happens. Not even when it happens does it happen, because you turn right around and bet again. And every time you lose. Stay away from horse folks — of any kind." She left, her walk slow and labored. This time when she closed her door the crockery didn't clatter.

Mindlessly, Elsa stared out the window. She had seen nothing amiss in their poverty. A torrent of rain beat against the house and drummed in her ears.

She hungered to see Wynn. Oh, God, how terribly lonely she was for her. Could a nickel make that much difference in what Mama handed over to those thieves each week? Elsa had no idea how much it was except for her own salary. *All* of it went to them. Them! For the thousandth time, she wondered exactly who "them" was.

Monday morning Elsa awoke to more pummeling rain and clawed away the blankets from her face where, sometime during the night, she had buried herself. A ruthless, throbbing pain engulfed her entire skull. Her teeth were clamped shut, and she spoke with drawn lips as she fought waves of nausea. "Mama," she called out. "Mama, help me. I'm sick."

She swung her feet over the edge of the bed. Her toes touched the floor. It felt as cold as a sheet of ice. Quickly drawing back her feet, she nearly threw up in the process.

Mama came in speaking sharply. "What is it? You'll be late for work. Now hurry up. Breakfast is already on the table."

"Mama, I'm sick." Sitting on the opposite side of the bed, Elsa tried to turn toward her mother, but any movement at all set her head clanging.

"You're not sick. You're spoiled. Now get up." She marched off.

Elsa's head drooped. "I'm sick, Mama," she moaned, but Mama was already slamming pots and pans around in the kitchen, each noise resounding like a church bell clobbering the inside of Elsa's skull.

She rose carefully, then remained very still until a strong dizzy spell had passed. Dressing with slow, careful movements, she avoided all unnecessary motion or bending and put on her favorite blue dress. She took the time to tie a scarf around her neck in a careful bow and gently brushed her hair, each stroke one of intense pain. She'd have to let her hair hang loose today. Pulling it back was out of the question.

She did most of her dressing with her eyes closed, then took a good look in the mirror to see that she didn't appear sick at all. She put on a big smile, ignoring the pain that even facial movements caused her.

Fighting increasing nausea, she placed both hands on the dresser and leaned closer to the mirror. "Maybe the one thing I did get from you, Papa, was determination. If you managed to hang onto this poor house, I guess I can get myself to work." She straightened up. "But this isn't for you, Papa. This is for me."

Sitting stiffly at the table, she forced down her breakfast, then washed her face, brushed her teeth, carefully applied her hat and left the house. Thankfully, Mama wasn't in a chatty mood this morning.

Her walk to work was a haze of excruciating pain, every step jarring her head, causing her unbearable agony, and she didn't know if she could keep down her breakfast.

She arrived on time and though she still had a raging headache, she smiled at every customer. She behaved cheerfully, acting more positively than she ever had before.

Gritting her teeth, she told herself she could behave like this every day. All she had to do was decide to do it.

Throughout the week her headaches and nausea continued, her discomfort never lessened, and her nights were pervaded with dreams of Wynn Carson. She tucked the dreams and her ailments into a small pouch somewhere inside her, making believe she was as happy as she had ever been. Now if only she could see Wynn. Elsa stuck that injury into her pouch with the others and ignored that one, too.

Uncomplaining, she handed Mama her salary the following Saturday. Mama began talking optimistically about how the debt was decreasing with all their hard work. Each Monday morning, she personally delivered the money to the creditors, wanting none of them coming near her house.

"Is there interest on this loan, Mama, like if you borrowed money from a bank?"

"There's interest. It's much higher than you'd ever pay at a bank, though."

"We'll be paying back for a long time."

Mama became irritated, her voice sharp. "You're forever complaining."

No, she wasn't, Elsa thought. Since deciding to change her attitude to a more positive one, she hadn't complained once. She had done everything asked of her with a smile on her face. Everything. But she wanted to quit now and just be the plain old self she knew she really was. As she thought about it, something within her wouldn't allow it. She'd carried on her farce for too long.

"You're right, Mama. I'll try not to whine anymore."

"See that you do."

Elsa went to the attic and thought only of Wynn.

CHAPTER SIX

During the following week the long rains had ended and spring had stepped in bold as brass. By the end of May, the weather on Staten Island had changed from dirty slush demanding heavy coats and hats to warm days needing light sweaters; green grass, appeared and birdsongs filled the air.

Bill Cody's Wild West Show was back on the island. Posters, lithographs and colored prints were plastered to every utility pole or free space available on the sides of buildings, barns and stores. Elsa couldn't possibly see the show, but its presence in town tugged at her heart, a constant hurtful reminder of Wynn. Without complaint on this Saturday evening, Elsa again pulled her pay envelope from her skirt pocket and laid it on the table beside the bills and coins Mama was already separating into various stacks.

Elsa watched her count out five more cents. Depression crushed her to a pulpy mass. "Please, Mama, I'd like some change for an omnibus so that I can go visit Wynn Carson." She looked around her. Did *she* ask that question? She hadn't even planned to ask Mama — ever. She was going to be a completely obedient daughter. She was going to avoid confrontations for the rest of her life.

Mama's eyes snapped angrily. "That show girl again. I thought you'd forgotten that trollop." She returned to counting money. "Don't be ridiculous, Elsa."

"Of course, Mama. I wasn't thinking." Elsa walked into her bedroom and paced back and forth. She could hear coins clinking together in the kitchen as she sat on the bed and clasped and unclasped her hands.

As the minutes passed, her resentment toward Mama, toward the thieves, grew. It became a ponderous thing, coiling itself around her, enclosing and suffocating her as it drew tighter and tighter around her mind. It wasn't possible for her to buy even a single penny stamp. Not one. Nor would she ever see Wynn again because five pennies kept them apart — for the next twenty years.

Animal-like, she growled low in her throat, like

the famished dogs snarling in the alley when they thought another animal might take what little food they'd managed to find.

She squeezed her eyes shut as hard as she could. Her muscles tightened to knots throughout her body. "I can't stand this anymore," she whispered, standing and slowly turning toward the door.

She ran to the kitchen where her envelope still lay unopened and seized it before her mother could stop her. "This money is mine. I earned it and I'm taking what I need."

Her mother leaped at her, lunging for the envelope. "Oh, no, you're not, young lady. Give me that." Much shorter than Elsa, she reached uselessly for the envelope held high overhead and out of reach. "Give me that, Elsa, right *now*."

Elbowing her mother aside, Elsa dumped the cash into her hand, laboring to extract ten cents.

Mama began to wail, then abruptly stopped tussling. "Fighting with my own daughter is insane," she cried. "All *right*, then! I'll quit taking your letters if you give back the money."

Else stiffened. "I figured there have been more. Did you read them?"

Mama returned to her accounts, wiping away flowing tears. "No, I never did that. I just burned them. Please give back the money."

Elsa studied her for a long time. She looked so small, so scared. Elsa felt heartless as she said, "You don't even care that you burned my letters do you, Mama?"

Mama's face tightened, her eyes shuttered as she looked at the ceiling and then at Elsa. "I care about living and about having a place to live in." She pleaded passionately, "Please give me the money, honey. We *need* it."

Elsa returned the envelope, saying, "*I* need this, Mama." She held up a balled fist tightly clutching a dime. "Don't fix me lunch for the week. That should make up for it."

"You must think about *them*," Mama hissed. She quaked as she glanced at the cash carefully sorted on the table.

Elsa started to respond, to give in, to hand Mama her single, piddling dime. Something within her rebelled as her mind returned to the days when her little bed was taken away, her davenport removed, the horse and buggy sold. "No, Mama. Not this time. And don't make any supper for me tonight."

Mama stood inflexible as a lamp post as Elsa left to get ready. Soon after, she waited outside the house to flag an omnibus, a daring thing for a young woman to do alone at this time of evening. Especially for her. She was thankful that daylight lingered much longer these days.

The driver let her off at Elsworth Avenue. She'd never traveled anywhere this far alone before. Not yet recovered from her fight with Mama, fear built upon fear as she looked around at the unfamiliar street. She wanted to run after the bus as it drew away, but an even more powerful drive to see Wynn pressed her forward.

The neighborhood was dismal and depressing. Refuse and animal excrement cluttered the sidewalks and gutters. The four-, five- and six-story buildings were old and worn, their brick facings dingy from age and every window gray with scum.

It was a warm evening. Adults lounged on porches

and hung from windows, calling to one another. Horses, buggies, dogs, cats and children were everywhere. The children screamed in joy as they played ball.

The building's interior was in equally poor condition. The wallpaper and carpeted and wooden floors were worn and colorless. Unpleasant cat and cooking odors permeated the hall.

Approaching Wynn's door, Elsa silently prayed, Please, God, it's been so awful long. Don't let her have moved away.

She knocked at Apartment Three, her knuckles barely making a sound against the door. Swallowing rapidly several times, she was unable to oust the lump sticking in her throat. A searing spasm in her belly doubled her. She breathed deeply and slowly until the paroxysm had passed and she could stand upright once again.

She knocked lightly a second time, afraid that Wynn would not be there and afraid that she would.

Soft footsteps approached from within. Elsa clutched her handbag until she crushed it.

The door opened a couple of inches, a chain lock restricting its swing.

"Wynn Carson?"

"Yes?" The horsewoman warily peered at Elsa.

At last, Wynn Carson stood before her. Only the probability of frightening her restrained Elsa from impulsively reaching out to touch her through the door's narrow opening. She could barely speak. "We've been writing to each other for several months. I'm Elsa Catulie." She smiled her well-practiced smile, feeling wrapped in a warm blanket of pleasure.

"You asked that I come and see you ride the next time your show came to town."

Wynn's eyes widened and a blush of rose colored her cheeks. "Yes, now I remember. Wait." She released the lock and opened the door. "How are you?" she asked. "My, I haven't heard from you in a long time. Come in, come in. Please don't mind the place. I didn't expect callers."

She stepped back as Elsa entered, saying, "It's nice to see you again." An explosive kernel of happiness settled in the center of Elsa's chest as Wynn led them to a tiny sitting room.

Elsa paled as she followed the trick rider. Wynn limped conspicuously, her left leg at least an inch shorter than her right. Elsa didn't remember Wynn hobbling. She couldn't recall Wynn's also missing several teeth on the upper left side of her mouth or her right arm hanging at a strange angle against her side. She wore a worn off-white Mother Hubbard dress. Old shoes covered her feet. There were no fancy clothes in sight. The change in Wynn was chilling.

The sitting room contained a couch and a small table upon which rested a chimney lantern. In one corner, a ladder-backed chair was burdened beneath a mound of unfinished ironing. Various posters of Wynn and her horse were randomly tacked to the walls. Interspersed among them were a few of Annie Oakley, William Cody and cowgirls and cowboys riding at great speeds.

They sat on the davenport. Wynn rested her hands in her lap, her smile as lovely as Elsa remembered, spoiled only by her missing teeth.

Wynn asked, "How have you been?"

It was difficult not to stare at Wynn's glaring afflictions. "I'm fine," Elsa said, keeping her tone light. "Working every day. Keeping busy. Too busy even to write to you like I first did."

Wynn nodded approvingly. "Steady work is a blessing. My work certainly wasn't steady."

Wasn't? No, Wynn wouldn't be able to do tricks in this condition. Elsa replied, "I don't expect it was. But, oh, the excitement of it. I can't imagine."

"It's not all fun." Wynn leaned back, laughing. "After we left here, we went to England on a ship so big that it had three masts. I thought it would be like riding in a rocking chair. I was never so wrong in my life. Everybody but the crew got seasick. I thought I was going to die. Even the men threw up all over the place. Big, tough roustabouts, cowboys and Indians all hanging over the railing together." She laughed heartily. "You should have seen them." She heaved a sigh and asked, "How's your family getting along?"

"We're doing fine," Elsa answered. "But, I have to say it, Wynn. You're plenty banged up since the last time I saw you." It was senseless not to acknowledge the trick rider's changes.

"Show business," Wynn answered flippantly. "I got hurt in Chicago last year. After I left the hospital I decided to move here, thinking I could get work right away. You know, lots of people, lots of employment. And I was familiar with the island already. I'd wandered around it a lot between shows."

"Don't you have family you could live with?"

"I do, but it's easier to stay here than go home and listen to Mother say, 'I told you so.' She'd say it enough times for my ears to fall off. Then I'd really look bad." She removed her shoes and tucked her feet beneath her dress. "I was supposed to live with a friend who'd help take care of me, but she married almost as soon as I moved nt. I met her the same way I met you. We wrote, became friends. But ..." She shrugged indifferently and looked around at her dreary surroundings, her eyes lingering on the posters.

"Do you ride anymore?"

"No. I just wash and iron and sew for people. There are a lot of dirty clothes out there." Wynn sighed again. This time she wasn't amused.

"Mama washes, too," Elsa said. "She gets very tired."

"So do I." Wynn chuckled softly. "I've had to learn to use my left hand. Right's pretty useless. I can still use my fingers some, but I can't lift a whole lot. I'm getting better, though. Stronger." Sorrow she could not hide invaded her eyes.

Placing her hand on Wynn's sleeve, Elsa detected a noticeable indentation midway of her forearm. "Wynn, you're badly hurt." It was repulsive touching the wound, adding to the nausea she still experienced. Struggling to appear calm, she left her hand in place. "May I ask what happened?"

Absently, Wynn put her hand over Elsa's. Elsa could feel the outline of the terrible disfigurement. Chills ran down her spine. Ashamed of her weakness, she wanted to withdraw her hand as if from a burning flame. If she did, Wynn would know in an instant how unpleasant her arm felt to Elsa.

Wynn breathed deeply before saying, "It was a wonderful show. The biggest ever. Mr. Cody brought in special guests. Annie Oakley shot her rifle. A cowboy rode a buffalo clear across the arena. Sitting Bull was there. I was considered the best trick rider." Wistfully, she said, "They all cheered for me, Elsa. They knew how good I was. I was so proud of what I did. My horse . . ." Her voice dropped, and her eyes filled with tears. "Buttons. They had to shoot my beloved Buttons. Do you remember him?"

Wynn's direct look and her obviously immense dismay infiltrated Elsa's heart. In a flash, she saw her father go down before her, never to laugh, to speak, to breathe again. Were she not so set on putting forward her new, cheery self, she would have crumbled like a dead leaf. "I remember him well. He was a beautiful friend."

"Yes, he was my friend. My best friend. He loved me no matter what."

"I'm sure others love you too, Wynn," Elsa said. Her hand remained sandwiched between Wynn's own and her friend's marked arm, her squeamishness slowly diminishing. She was proud that she hadn't withdrawn her hand. Wynn clearly needed to talk more than Elsa needed to run. A thought dashed through her mind. Who did Wynn chat with when she needed a friend? A thread of ownership struck her. Elsa wanted to be the one.

"Not like Buttons did." Anguish lingered in Wynn's hazel eyes. "I rode perfectly that night. Not a mistake. Buttons and I were like one animal . . . or one human, I'm not sure which. I was never sure with him." She looked again at the posters on the walls.

"I once loved a horse like that," Elsa said. And then Papa had sold him.

"Some people think I'm crazy."

"You're not." Elsa studied Wynn's tired eyes. A rush of feeling, elemental and alien, pleasantly struck her.

"It was my last swing around the arena. We were floating on air. I hung upside down from my saddle terrifying the audience. They were screaming their heads off. But I'd done it so many times before, I knew I was perfectly safe. And then...a lady...a rich lady, I suppose, sitting in the front row, draped her fur coat over the railing just as we got there. Guess she was hot, or something. It was September, for Christ's sake." Wynn stopped speaking. She seemed to stop breathing as well.

"Wynn?"

Wynn blinked, returning from her reverie. "Buttons panicked. He probably thought a bear was coming at him. He shied away from the coat and stumbled. I was trying to hang on for dear life. He fell. I fell. He broke his leg. I broke my arm and leg and smashed my face." She smiled brightly. "I don't look too bad though, do I?"

"No," Elsa answered truthfully. "You look quite lovely."

Wynn lapsed into her previous mood. "I can't ride anymore."

"You can still ride, Wynn." Elsa took Wynn's hand in her own. A pleasant hammer blow hit her in the chest as she felt the thick calouses still there. She said, "You just can't do tricks anymore."

"Tricks are what made the riding fun for me, Elsa. Anybody can sit a saddle and hang on."

Elsa laughed. Her rides on Papa's horse hadn't all been successes. "I remember falling off a couple of times, and I was hanging on." About as tight as she was holding onto Wynn's hand. She loosened her grip.

Wynn shifted and resettled herself. "When you really have to, you do, provided you're not hanging upside down from a running horse who thinks a bear is after him."

They both laughed lightly, Elsa sensing that Wynn had said enough about her difficulties and wished to move on to other things. Elsa released her, feeling the moment for handholding had passed.

Wynn prepared tea which they sipped from cracked china cups, and they spent the next couple of hours exchanging stories of their lives. Wynn thought Elsa lived a sheltered but secure life. Elsa, on the other hand, believed that Wynn should be envied for her countless adventures and opportunities.

"But," Wynn concluded, "not having to pack up and move every month or so and sleeping in my very own bed every night isn't bad at all."

Elsa brushed aside a strand of hair, which she'd not yet been able to roll into a bun. It irritated her, the hair constantly in her eyes and tickling her cheeks. "I still think it would be exciting to have done even half the things you have."

"There are a few women around who ride broncos and bulls and rope calves. Some are very good barrel racers and relay riders where they get to make believe they're pony express riders."

"And now they're all dead, too."

"Only a few." Wynn guffawed. "The rest limp like me."

"I've been on a gentle horse. He jumped a few fences for me, but nothing dangerous." Elsa felt a bit ashamed that she hadn't just about broken her neck at least once while riding.

"I could teach you saddle tricks." Wynn leaped from the davenport nearly tumbling over her own feet. "Darn," she said, laughing. "Gotta practice that one some more."

They giggled themselves silly, Elsa deeply admiring Wynn's courage and willingness to laugh at herself.

"No, thanks. I'm satisfied with just plain old-fashioned riding where I get to stay in the saddle and hang onto the horn if I want to."

"There's good money in bronco riding. Not much to it except to hang on."

Elsa's ears pricked up. Then her wisdom took over. "I'd get killed first thing."

"Oh, you wouldn't be allowed to ride." Wynn pointed to one of the posters. "Those women are professionals. Most of them come from ranches or farms and have been breaking horses for years."

"I don't believe you. Girls don't do that kind of work. It would kill us."

Wynn looked askance at Elsa, clearly amused by her innocence. "The men don't have the time. They're usually out chasing cows. Out West, women break horses all the time and don't give it a thought."

"Such hard work," Elsa said, amazed. "How can the men allow it?"

"If they're not there, somebody has to. Men don't think much about their women working hard. It's just something that everybody does. Even the kids by the time they're five or six, are doing some kind of work. Bringing in wood, feeding chickens. Stuff like that. And the women bronco riders think they're making real easy money. To them it's just another job. The difference is that they collect twenty-five dollars each time they ride a full ride and put on one hell of a show doing it."

"Twenty-five dollars. Imagine. How long do you have to stay on?"

"Official time is eight seconds."

"That's all? That's not much."

"Then there's second and third prize for fifteen and ten dollars. It's still pretty good money."

"More than I make in a month. But what an idea." Elsa's vision blurred as she let her mind run rampant. The crowd cheered wildly, shouting her name over and over. She rode like the wind. The big, feral horse bucked like the Hudson River gone mad. She stayed in the saddle the whole time. She won! She would be given her money as soon as she got off the horse. The horse! She turned to Wynn. "How do you stop the horse?"

"A cowboy on horseback rides up and you grab him and he grabs you. You let go of the bronco, and the cowboy drops you to the ground."

Some man grabbing at her? She checked her watch. Regrefully, she said, "I'd better go. Work starts early tomorrow. You need your rest, too."

"I suppose." Wynn sounded tired and suddenly looked melancholy.

Together, they walked to the door. Wynn gave Elsa a long, warm hug, her healthy arm holding Elsa close, her injured one resting across Elsa's shoulder. "I'm so glad you came, Elsa. I haven't had a real good talk with anybody in a long time."

Wynn's hair teased Elsa's nose and cheek. She

found it curious that she didn't notice the tickling sensation to be at all irritating the way it was when her own hair got in her way.

Wynn clasped Elsa tighter still. "I hope you'll stop by again sometime."

"I'll try," Elsa answered. She'd be back. If she had to rip the money right out of those men's hands who controlled her very life, she'd get it, and she'd be back!

Wynn let her go. There were tears in her eyes. "You don't suppose we could go to the Wild West show, do you? It'll be here a whole month."

Elsa's eyebrows shot up. She hadn't given it a thought. "I don't know. How much are the tickets?"

"Five dollars."

Elsa blanched, but held her internal ground. "Maybe. I'll see. I'll at least come back to let you know."

Wynn looked off into space somewhere. "I used to be a star. Now people stare at me because I walk funny. My smile's a disaster. I used to be pretty. Beautiful, some said." She faced Elsa. "I guess that still makes me a star then, if folks are still gawking at me, doesn't it?" She attempted a smile, but it quickly faded.

"You'll always be a star, Wynn, for as long as you believe it. And if you believe it, that's all that really matters." Elsa patted Wynn on the shoulder, not as daring as Wynn in initiating a hug.

"You're right. I should think like you do. That's a nice way to be."

But I'm not, Elsa wanted to cry out. I pretend I'm happy, but I'm really sad all the time and I don't even know why. Not right now, though. Not at this moment. "I'm glad you think so," she said. "I'll see you as soon as I can. Don't look for letters. Seeing you in person is best." No sense in telling Wynn how poor she was. Wynn didn't look to be in much better shape herself.

Wynn stood on her tiptoes and placed a delicate kiss on Elsa's cheek.

Elsa didn't dare return the kiss, but she would get that money. Oh, she'd get it. And then she and Wynn would go to the Wild West show.

Wynn waited outside with her until Elsa caught a bus. They said goodbye once more, using only their eyes this time.

CHAPTER SEVEN

During the next few days, Elsa agonized over how she might buy a ticket. It wasn't just the price of admission. She was obsessed with the idea of how she could get her hands on enough cash for an entrance fee. She wanted to ride a bronco. No, that wasn't true. She didn't want to ride any berserk horse, but the twenty-five-dollar first place prize money made the idea powerfully inviting. That much cash would go far in paying off Papa's debt, every cent freeing them just a little more. The idea consumed her.

She sat quietly in the attic. It was still a peaceful

place, but these days she rested on a soap box while Papa's trunk of untruths still lay in a shambles at her feet. She ignored the clutter as she watched the night slowly descend upon the neighborhood.

Since visiting Wynn the week before, her headache and nausea had disappeared. Suddenly both were back as she closed her eyes and considered the possibilities of obtaining some swift cash. She could ask for a raise. That would never work. Miss Ashley would say no, and laugh. She could refuse to give up her salary for a week. Again, a bad idea. It would throw Mama into a prime mad-dog fit.

One thought lay hidden deep within her. The notion had skated across her imagination earlier, and before it became even slightly lucid, Elsa blotted it out. Now, though, alone in the semi-darkness with no one nearby to disrupt her other than a tiny spider crawling across the wall and a mouse occasionally darting in and out of a ragged hole near the door, she retrieved the concept from some dark, forbidden place buried deep within her.

She sat fixed as a cat as the idea took hold and grew. Her body chilled and her headache and nausea spiraled as the possibility of its success magnified. Sweat began to soak her underarms and roll down her sides. She was no longer in the attic, but rather, somewhere else, concealing the money in her hand.

"Elsa, come on down now. Help me clean up the kitchen."

Mama's voice bit sharply into her musing, and she shook her head as though waking from a nightmare. "All right, Mama." She wiped sweating palms against her skirt as the spell and her sickness disintegrated.

Thank God Mama had called her. She was free of deliberation and free to think rationally again.

The following morning, Elsa waited on her last patron before going to lunch. "Thank you very much," she said pleasantly to the middle-aged woman. The lady gathered her packages, and Elsa watched her leave.

She glanced around. No one seemed to be nearby right now. Her heartbeat became ungovernable as she moved to the cash register. She hadn't quite closed it during her last sale, a detail Miss Ashley continuously harped upon and had never once found Elsa derelict in. For the first time since working here, she was.

Her throat muscles tightened, but she ignored the unnerving feeling and moved back to the drawer.

Maintaining her poise, she opened the drawer a bit wider. Another quick check. No one looked her way. The floor walker was at the far end of the building if he was maintaining his customary schedule of circling the store's interior parameter before lacing his way back through the aisles.

She scanned the place once more, pretending she was looking for a potential shopper while at the same time slipping her hand into the till and lifting two coins, a ten-dollar gold piece and a quarter dollar. She balled the change in her clammy palm and gently closed the drawer.

When she looked up, Miss Ashley stood not five yards away, staring at her. Horrifying shockwaves ripped through her as Ashley continued scrutinizing her. In fact, Elsa noted, the woman was staring right through her. No, not through her, past her. Still stricken, Elsa turned to see what had caught her eye.

A tall, well-dressed, lightly bearded man as handsome as Elsa had ever seen was gazing right back at Miss Ashley.

She sped past Elsa, not stopping until she reached the attractive man who held out his arm. They left the store and disappeared from Elsa's sight.

She expelled a ragged breath, leaning heavily against the counter for several seconds, waiting for her nerves to stop quaking and her lightheadedness to pass. Miss Ashley had seen nothing.

Elsa rammed the sweat-soaked coins deep into her skirt pocket, vowing never again to steal another thing no matter how desperate she was, and she'd go to confession Saturday night.

With trembling hands, she gathered her lunch and joined several other salesgirls already out gossiping behind the store. A few benches were randomly located beneath a large sugar maple tree. Putting on the bravest front she had ever rendered, Elsa chose a spot between two salesgirls and yakked right along with them as though she had done nothing wrong, hadn't stolen from the till, hadn't broken the law; hadn't shamed herself and her parents, hadn't broken a Commandment. She smiled her practiced smile and swallowed her tasteless food, conducting herself in a righteous manner consistent with all she had been taught to believe was correct and proper.

That evening, she grasped Wynn in a powerful embrace as soon as the door closed behind them. Wynn's warmth and softness invaded her senses. She savored the tranquility and security the woman's arms provided.

"Aren't we frisky this evening?" There was laughter in Wynn's voice.

Elsa released her and stepped back, her hands remaining on Wynn's shoulders. "How about going to see the show tonight."

"Tonight?" Wynn paused only briefly. "Why not? I was sewing. I hate sewing. Let's go."

During the omnibus ride there, Wynn commented, "You look better this evening, Elsa. Healthier, like you'd put on weight over the past few days, or something."

Elsa smiled, replying happily, "Thank you. I'm feeling quite good today."

She wasn't. She was miserable and scared out of her mind. And she hadn't put on weight at all.

Beneath her dress she wore clothing stolen from Mama's bedroom the minute she went to the backhouse this evening: Papa's suit pants, the legs rolled up and tucked into his boots with cloth scraps stuffed in the toes to make them fit, his blue denim work shirt and his hat. She carried no purse and felt naked without it. She was uncomfortable and hot and sick to her stomach, unsure that she could go through with this insane plan.

They found seats halfway up the bleachers. "Pretty good view from here," Elsa said.

"Better one from down there." Wynn looked longingly at the arena grounds where dozens of show people were lining up to begin the parade.

"You're right," Elsa agreed. "I wish you were there, too." She patted Wynn's thigh and felt her leg muscles ripple. The woman was strong! What a tragic shame she could no longer be a trick rider.

As soon as the procession began, Elsa said, "I've got to go to the outhouse."

"You'll miss the parade."

"Can't be helped." Elsa's face reddened. "When it's time for me, it's time for me. Don't worry if I'm gone too long. Just don't go anywhere."

"Take all the time you need."

That's exactly what Elsa would be taking: eight seconds of it if she lived long enough.

She found the women's outhouses well behind and away from the stands. There were several in a row with long lines stretching before each of them.

Hidden from view, spectators clapped and yelled wildly for somebody shooting and breaking glass balls. Restlessly, she rocked from one foot to the other as the women slowly entered and exited and dwelled only on what she must do next and that was to patiently wait in this preposterously long line until it was her turn.

At last she entered an outhouse, bolting the door behind her. The place stank. She breathed through her mouth as little as possible, the tiny room dreadfully confining and hot.

Struggling to work within the scanty space, Elsa removed her hat and dress, clasping them between her knees. She grabbed Papa's crumbled hat from inside the shirt and pulled it down as low and as tight as she could, shoving her hair up under it. She stuffed her own clothing into the shirt, toiling with the bulky material until it encircled her waist, chest and back. She crammed plenty into her pants, too. She'd need it there for sure.

She patted herself, making sure the dress laid as flat as possible. Satisfied she'd done all she could do in the dark, cheerless room, she took a deep breath.

She wheeled immediately, hanging her head over the hole and vomiting. Sickening fumes influenced additional retching. She pinched her nostrils to slow the uncontrollable spasms. Eventually, she could stand upright again.

Exiting the hellish room, she wiped away tears, vomit and sweat with the back of Papa's sleeve. She sucked in fresh air while waiting women looked strangely at her. "Is that a man?" they murmured. Elsa ignored the whispered comments as she stumbled away.

At first chance, she collapsed on the ground against a stack of hay. The aroma of fresh cut grass was the best thing she'd ever smelled, and she breathed in the gratifying fragrance and cleansed her nostrils of the stench still lingering there. Closing her eyes, she lay back and stretched out her legs in a most unladylike position. Her hands lay limp beside her while she gathered renewed strength and concentration. She was unmindful of people strolling by staring at her and horses and riders making their way back and forth kicking up dust and grit, soiling her clothes. The earth's common smells were a blessing.

According to her watch, she must get to the entry office and sign up. The bronco event was coming up soon.

Standing with effort and walking as though she meant every step, she found the office and the man in charge of entry fees. Laying her money on his desktop, she said, "I'm with the show. I'm riding a bronc." She stood as tall as she could.

"Who are you?"

A name! She needed a name, not just a too-large man's shirt and pants to hide her identity. She scrambled for something obscure. "Mary Smith."

The man looked at her doubtfully. "From?"

"Kentucky."

He scribbled down the information in a ledger. "Had two Mary Smiths here last week. One from Arizona, other from Ohio. Any relation?"

"None."

He looked her over. "You're tall enough, but you're kinda plump. Didn't know Cody hired such."

She rested her hidden lanky frame against the wall much as she had seen men do. Tossing her head in the direction of the corrals, she said, "Mister, I can ride anything you got over there." Muscular, compact horses pranced and paced restlessly, nipping at each other's hides and lashing out with small, irritating kicks at other horses who came too close. They all looked killing mean.

"Lemme see your grip."

He stuck out a large hand. She stared at it unsure of what to do.

"Lady, you say you ride for Cody. Lemme see your grip. That'll tell me if you can at least hold the reins. We don't want any locals sneaking in and getting killed out there. Bad for business."

She respectfully took his hand.

"You ain't no rider, missy. Get going. Cody's girls'll put you to shame." He turned to give his attention to another young woman who had come up behind Elsa. "Now here's what I call a real bronc girl."

The girl had to be at least six feet tall, weighing two hundred pounds. Her cheek muscles twitched and her dark eyes bore into Elsa's as she glanced her way. She returned her attention to the man.

"Howdy." Her voice was seven octaves lower than Elsa's. She also had no front teeth.

The man peered around the big woman's shoulder. "This is the kinda girl rides here, lady. Go on back home to your knitting."

The woman hitched up her pants and pulled a well-seasoned hat lower over her eyes. She plunked down her money, and the man signed her up without hesitation.

Elsa watched the hulking woman move with fearless confidence. "Here, now," she proclaimed, dropping her voice as low as possible. "You wanna grip my hand, then grip my darn hand." She elbowed the immense woman aside. "Grip it, mister, and then give me my number."

His eyebrows arched as a wry smile peeked out from beneath his unkempt beard. "Get outta here, darlin'."

"Grab it." She thrust out her hand.

Roaring with amusement, he accommodated her. His hand was big as a bear's paw, thick with calluses and age.

She pressed with all her might. The man squeezed back but she stayed with him. She could feel her fingers being crushed together, the sweat from both their grips acting as a lubricant. She stared unflinchingly into his eyes, preventing her fingers from collapsing for as long as possible, enduring the sadistic pain he inflicted upon her.

At last he released her and guffawed again. "Okay, lady. Now lemme see your other hand."

She could stick out her left hand and come away with nothing left to hang onto the horse with or she could call his bluff — like she suspected Papa would do. "Nuts to you, mister. You got all you're getting."

Still laughing, he said, "Gimme a fiver. Pin your number on your back. Your relay's coming up in ten minutes."

Her eyes smoldering, she pocketed her change and started toward the chutes. The big woman tagged alongside her. "Good for you. He ain't nothin' but a bull's asshole."

Elsa's ears burned. She increased her stride to rid herself of the unwelcomed companion.

"You rode before?" the woman asked.

"I ain't a first-time rider," Elsa snapped.

"If you ain't, you better ride like you ain't then, girl, or they'll disqualify you straight outten the chute."

The woman ambled off toward the stalls. Elsa paused to let her go ahead.

A couple of minutes later, Elsa sat frozen on Chute C's upper rail, her number flapping slightly in the wind. She'd be riding third in this relay. Below her, a cowboy cinched the restless stallion's saddle. "You want the stirrups tied?" he asked.

"Tied?"

"You rode before, lady?"

"Who ain't?" she quipped.

"So, you want the stirrups tied down or not?"

"Might's well. Take advantage of everything I can." The cowboy bent beneath the horse.

"Number eight!" an announcer called out. "Jane Morson of Texas on Powderkeg."

Two chutes over, Elsa watched the gate swing

wide. Rider and horse slowly emerged from the pen. For three seconds, nothing happened, the woman and her mount looking as serene as though just beginning a Sunday ride. Abruptly the peace was split as the horse screamed and jackknifed, coming straight up off the ground and landing stiffly on all four hooves. Space appeared between the woman and her saddle before she could grab the horn. Her stirrups were tied or she would already have been dislodged from the saddle. She stuck to the leather for another couple of seconds before being thrown and landing squarely on her back. A mounted cowboy raced up to her and quickly dismounted. The woman was out cold. A second cowboy galloped after the bronco and lassoed him. The horse meekly followed his captor back to the corral.

Elsa looked again at the downed rider. She was just sitting up and struggling to breathe. The man got her to her feet and a great cheer went up, but what Elsa observed was the way the heroic rider staggered from the arena. She almost went down once, but the cowboy caught her and kept her upright until they exited the grounds.

Behind the chutes, she collapsed at his feet. "You'll be okay," he told her. "You just ain't breathing right yet." He left her and returned to the arena.

Elsa stared in horror at the injured woman. She wasn't making any attempt to move.

Chute B's rider and horse was announced and the door opened. It was the big woman Elsa had seen earlier. She succeeded in staying in the saddle until a

71

earlier. She succeeded in staying in the saddle until a cowboy pulled her off. Elsa was filled with sheer terror, and her knees turned to jelly.

"Your turn, twelve." The cowboy touched her shoe.

Overwhelming panic gripped her. Here was the horse. Here was the arena. It was time to ride. In much less than a minute she would be no more.

"Mount up, lady. We got five more riders waiting behind you." He scowled at her, muttering impatiently, "Bunch a' assholes, these girls. Ain't worth it."

No one had ever called her such a horrid name. Even Miss Ashley was more pleasant to her than that!

She vaulted from the railing and landed heavily and clumsily in the saddle. The horse grunted under the unexpected thrust of weight on his back. He rolled his eyes and laid back his ears, as she rammed her feet into the stirrups and grabbed his chin rope.

"Hey, lady, ease into the saddle on these heathens. Christ, a'mighty, you some kinda dummy or something?"

The horse stomped his hooves and snorted loudly as rider number twelve, Mary Smith from Kentucky on Ramrod's Dream, was announced.

She yanked her hat down hard as the door swung wide. "Get outta my way, cowboy."

CHAPTER EIGHT

The horse came out of the chute at a dead run, snapping Elsa backwards and nearly yanking her from the saddle. Hidden strength abiding somewhere within enabled her to right herself before the horse began bucking. She clutched at the rope with both hands to adjust her seat, then single-handedly held on with a puissant grip while her free arm flew back and forth across her chest.

The crowd cheered wildly. Catcalls and whistles, shouts of encouragement and of death echoed throughout the bleachers.

But Elsa couldn't hear them. Only audible was her own loud, involuntary grunts with each powerful movement of the volcanic demon vaulting beneath her and his snorting and blowing exhibiting his savage displeasure.

Spectators, the earth beneath her, the surrounding fence, the mounted cowboy hovering nearby to save her very life were a blur. She could distinguish nothing clearly except the horn on her saddle screaming at her to grab it and live and the horse's mane thrashing about, some of the hairs flailing her face if she leaned too far forward. Sweltering, dusty soil saturated with odors of horse sweat and manure pervaded her lungs.

Several times, the stallion spun to his left, throwing her far to the right. Desperately she adjusted her weight and stayed on. Once he arched his neck so high during a particularly fierce leap, he tossed Elsa forward and nearly over his head. Only the blow against her forehead from contact with the bronco knocked her back into the saddle, seating her upright again.

Repeatedly, her neck and spine were snapped into painful, unnatural positions. Each time she was slammed onto the rock-hard leather seat, a deluge of excruciating agony filled her bottom. Already, the insides of her thighs were chafed from her pants.

Her booted feet whipped wildly back and forth as if to spur the animal into even more frenzied leaping and bucking. An experienced rider encouraged this in his mount, Wynn had told her, but for Elsa, it was a matter of balancing herself so that she could just stay on this insane monster.

She stuck with him for what seemed like another

three years before a strong arm grabbed her in a powerful grip. The arm roughly yanked her from the saddle and dropped her to the ground. Her knees nearly gave way. The cowboy retriever whooped, "Best ride yet. You're in the running for sure. You want to ride back with me?"

She wavered unsteadily, unable to bend her neck properly to look up at him.

The cowboy dismounted. "Can you walk outta here by yourself?"

She nodded weakly and he mounted up and cantered off.

By some miracle, she still wore her hat. She pulled it tight again and wobbled out of the arena, listening to the roaring mob. She stayed around watching the remaining riders while slowly rubbing the kinks out of her neck and catching her breath. The prizes would be given out immediately afterward.

A few minutes later she was declared the winner and awarded twenty-five dollars. Collecting her prize at the winner's gate, she couldn't even enjoy her victory she hurt so.

The big woman was there, too. She sauntered over. "Hell of a ride, honey. Wanna go get a beer and talk about it?"

"Later, maybe." The nervy woman unsettled Elsa, making her feel *pursued* somehow. She stuffed the precious money into her pocket and headed back to the outhouses, feeling the woman's penetrating eyes following her.

Dear God, she couldn't wait until this whole sordid mess was over and done with. She still needed to replace what she'd stolen. In addition, Mama must *never* find out about tonight. Sometime when Mama wasn't around, she'd slip her extra winnings into the money jar.

The lines were still as long at the outhouses. "You belong over to the men's outhouses, sir." A tired, gaunt woman unmercifully tugged on by a small boy looked suspiciously and disapprovingly at Elsa.

"I'm a lady," Elsa replied. At least she used to be. She removed her hat and shook her hair loose. Her head was drenched with sweat. "I'm with the show." It was only a half lie.

"Oh." The beleaguered woman turned her back on Elsa, obviously dismissing her as an improper female.

Elsa mentally scanned her body. Oh, how she hurt — everywhere. Even the tips of her toes were injured, rubbed raw from their continuous jamming against the rags in the ill-fitting boots.

She took a deep breath and gasped. Gingerly touching her ribs, she winced with pain. If she didn't know better, she'd bet she'd cracked one or two. She took no more deep breaths.

Inside the outhouse, she pulled her money out of her pocket and held it with her teeth while she rid herself of Papa's clothing, tossing it down the hole. Mama would wonder whatever became of his things, but Elsa would deny everything. The boots she'd have to return.

She was instantly awash with guilt. Papa's clothes had helped her win tonight. But, she argued with herself, she wouldn't have had to wear them at all and nearly kill herself in the process if it hadn't been for him.

Although her clothing and hat were a crumpled

mess, the glorious comfort of their familiar cut and shape felt like the loving pat of a mother's hand as she put them on.

As consoled as she might be by being herself again, she was overcome by the pain and the wretched odors wafting up from the hole, a hundred times worse now that several thousand more women and children had used it. She came to, crammed between the seat and the door, the money still riveted between her teeth. Using the door handle, she pulled herself to her feet, her ribs screaming in protest.

Pocketing her cash, she threw open the door. Only ruthless discipline kept her moving as she walked painfully back through the crowd and climbed to her seat.

Wynn smiled. "Hi, there. Are you all right? A half dozen times I wanted to check up on you." She slid over to make room. "You were gone forever. What happened?"

"Long lines. Very long lines." Elsa tried to pay attention to the activities going on around her. As she gingerly sat, needling pain pierced her tailbone upon contact with the hard plank seat. She stifled a groan but was unable to refrain from grimacing.

"People are still coming in," Wynn said. "Can you believe this?" Her legs pressed against Elsa's who took comfort in their closeness. Wynn didn't try to move away, and Elsa needed the physical support Wynn unknowingly gave her.

She cleared her throat as another wave of pain attacked her ribs. She thought she sounded almost normal.

"You missed the bronco riding," Wynn said.

Elsa fixed her eyes on the rope-calving event going on. "Is that so?"

"You didn't miss much. Nobody rode very well. Couple of women got thrown. Another got her brains slammed in by not using them." Wynn laughed at her own joke.

A surge of fear struck Elsa. Did her forehead have a black and blue mark on it? If it did, it'd be the size of an apple. Nonchalantly, she reached up to pull her bonnet and some strands of hair over her possible, and likely, bruise.

Eventually the rodeo was over. They remained seated until most spectators had dispersed. Wynn asked, "Want to go meet the show people. I know a lot of them."

"You go. I'll wait."

While Wynn was gone, Elsa contented herself staying where she was. Not moving for hours would be nice. When Wynn returned a great splash of a smile divided her face, and her eyes glistened brightly. She sat beside Elsa. "It was great seeing old friends again. I miss them." She paused and then asked, "You ready to leave?"

Elsa nodded. Standing upright took away her breath. Her ribs flared and she stifled an agonizing groan. The backs of her legs had tightened to twisted knots. The tenacity with which she controlled her battered body created a dreadful headache. Movement caused nausea. She sat again enduring the expected shooting pain up her spine, and breathed as deeply as she dared.

Wynn studied her. "Elsa, are you okay?" She put

a hand to Elsa's forehead. "You don't seem to be fevered."

Apparently, Wynn detected no knot and no black and blue mark. Evidently Papa's hat had protected her. Elsa was cranky and tired to death of the Wild West show. "Let's just go."

Wynn stiffened. "Elsa, look at me."

Elsa wouldn't. She wanted only to leave.

Wynn grasped Elsa's wrist. "You rode tonight, didn't you? Am I right? Were you number twelve?"

"What if I was?"

"Never mind 'what.' I want to know why."

Elsa shamefully dropped her eyes. "I need the money — desperately."

Wynn shook her head. "You're crazy."

Elsa already knew that.

"Are you hurt? I saw you knocked silly."

Elsa confessed at a whisper. "Broke a rib, I think."

"Come on, we've got to get you home." Wynn's voice held a nervous edge. She helped Elsa stand and assisted her off the bleachers. Riding the crowded omnibus, Elsa ignored the other passengers and rested her head against the window.

Wynn babbled at a whisper to her all the way back to her apartment. "You could have gotten arrested, if not killed. Whatever made you do it? What'd you do, steal your father's clothes? You changed in the outhouse, didn't you? My word, girl. Don't *ever* do that again."

"Furthest thing from my mind," Elsa assured her. Her head drooped forward, and she fell into a light sleep.

She heard Wynn say, "We're here."

"I've got to go home. It's late."

"Who cares? Come in first. I can fix you up so you'll feel better."

"Mama cares."

"I care, too. Come with me."

Elsa debated going home or following Wynn. Mama would yell because she was late. Wynn said she could make Elsa feel better. She followed Wynn.

Wynn's bedroom was furnished with a single bed, a small table beside it and a bureau and mirror. She lighted a couple of lamps. "Lie down while I make us some tea."

A few minutes later a kettle whistled. Shortly after, Wynn delivered two steaming cups of tea on a tray, holding one side with her able hand and balancing the other with her injured arm. She set the tray beside the bed.

Elsa rose on an elbow to reach for hers and gasped, "I can't sit." Sweat poured from her brow as she lay back.

"Can I check your side?"

Elsa nodded and Wynn probed here and there, cautiously running her fingertips over Elsa's ribs. "Does it hurt here when I press?"

"No."

Wynn tried a couple more places, each time Elsa denying any pain. "It's only when I move or breathe."

"You've hurt yourself. Can't deny that, but I don't think it's your ribs. You'd have been screaming if they were. You've just pulled some muscles pretty bad."

"Feels like broken ribs. Dozens of them."

"How about a horse liniment rubdown?"

"That's all right. Anyway, I'd stink to high heaven and have to answer all kinds of questions at home."

"You're going to stiffen up like a butchered steer if you don't at least have a rubdown. Leave your dress on if you're shy, and we'll begin with your back."

"Go ahead." Elsa struggled to roll over.

CHAPTER NINE

Wynn started with the muscles in Elsa's neck and shoulders, the healthy fingers of her left hand slowly working their way down Elsa's back and arms to her palms which didn't ache. Using her bad hand, she caressed Elsa's back in broad, circular strokes, lightly kneading her smooth skin. "This is a good workout for my fingers," she said as Elsa luxuriated in her first ever body-rub.

"Mm, that feels good."

"I'm an expert. I've given lots of rubdowns." Wynn moved downward to Elsa's buttocks.

"Hey!"

"What? You're not hurt here?"

"Yes, I hurt there. I hurt all over."

"Then relax and let Dr. Carson do her work. It's only more muscle, Elsa, for crying out loud."

Elsa certainly wanted to relax. Wynn was making her feel funny where she wasn't used to feeling funny. It wasn't exactly a relaxing type of sensation. It made her feel more like she wanted to push her hips into the mattress.

Wynn continued kneading Elsa's bottom for a minute or so longer, then moved up and down the length of her body while quietly humming a soft tune. She said, "Elsa, I really need to pull up your skirt. There's just too much cloth here for me to do your legs right."

"My legs, too?"

"Well," Wynn answered a little impatiently. "They're your legs and it's your pain."

Elsa breathed into the pillow. "Go ahead." It'd be embarrassing, but it'd be better to get rid of the pain.

Wynn drew Elsa's skirt to just above her hips and put her hands on her thighs. Her fingers knew just where to concentrate. Her voice muffled by the pillow, Elsa asked, "How do you know where the sore spots are?"

"By the color of your skin. A black spot here. A blue one there. I work around them, and it's a good workout for my fingers."

She worked toward Elsa's inner thigh area. The chafing from Papa's pants was no longer noticeable. An unusual heat gathered around Elsa's waist and just a little below that. The warmth wasn't like heat from the kitchen stove or the summer sun. It was more . . . penetrating. "I've never had a rubdown before. Those horses sure are lucky devils."

"You've decided you like it?"

"I've decided to become a horse. They get rubdowns more often than I ever will."

"I could give you one when you come visit next time." Wynn's hands paused. "Will you come over again?"

"As soon as I can."

"I'll be here." She slapped Elsa smartly on the rump. "Turn over."

Elsa yelped. "That hurt, Wynn."

"You said you wanted to be a horse. That's what I do to horses."

Elsa lay flat on her back. "Horses don't hurt like I do. I don't want to be a horse if that's how you treat them. It's cruel."

"I'll begin with your head." Wynn went briskly about her business, first massaging Elsa's scalp, then her temples and finally her cheeks.

Elsa felt her face being stretched this way and that. "I must look like a clown when you do that."

"You do. But a lovely clown."

"Liar."

"I am not lying. You are lovely."

"I hate a liar, Wynn. Real bad." Hostility welled up within her, volcanic and ready to erupt.

"I'm not lying."

"Then you see something I hardly ever saw."

"Look in the mirror more often then, silly. You'll see."

Studying herself in her mirror at home, Elsa had occasionally thought she looked almost pretty, but she was never fully convinced that she actually was. Long face, long nose, thin lips. That's mostly what she saw.

"You remind me of a fine English lady I once knew." Wynn's hands continued working their magic on Elsa's body.

"Where is she now?"

"She went back to England — with an American husband."

"Sounds like you miss her."

"Not so bad anymore."

"It's hard to lose friends."

"Or fathers."

How compassionate Wynn was. Elsa suddenly saw her in a much different light. She had become stunningly beautiful. Her missing teeth couldn't be seen. Her gimpy arm was straight; both hands were equally strong. "I see you as perfect," Elsa said.

"Don't talk like a drunken cowhand at the beer booth."

"I'm not. You look perfect to me. And you talk pretty."

"Stop." Wynn spoke sharply causing blood to rush to Elsa's head and embarrassing tears to spring to her eyes.

"Quit that crying, too. I can't stand a weepy woman."

Elsa swallowed her tears. "Women cry."

"Only when they need to. Not over something like this. I'm not perfect. I'm not even pretty anymore. You know it. I know it. All that's gone." She gave Elsa's chin a sharp pinch.

"Ouch! All right, you're an ugly, old hag not worth a forkful of horse manure." Hurt, and piqued that her compliments had been thrown in her face, Elsa added, "You're uppity and blank-headed. And you're not very nice. How's that?"

"That's more like it."

Elsa simmered as Wynn's hands worked their magic. Wynn was perfect enough for Elsa. Very, very lovely, she thought.

"If I were a whole person again . . ."

Elsa sat up quickly. "Ahhh." She fell back, the sweat pouring down her face.

"Lay still, you fool."

Able only to whisper at the moment, Elsa said, "You're a whole person, Wynn. If you believe anything else, you're the fool. Even I know that much."

"In a minute I'll know how much."

Elsa puzzled over her comment.

Wynn's eyes closed slowly as her nostrils flared. Wynn began kneading Elsa's belly. An exquisite inferno raged within as Wynn's fingers rhythmically opened and closed on her. "You're certainly soft, aren't you?"

Unable to reply as a series of tiny deep jolts attacked several of her tummy muscles, Elsa pinched her eyes shut. "Wynn, maybe I've had enough. I'm beginning to tense up quite a bit."

Wynn's hand moved away from Elsa's stomach slipping to the top of Elsa's private place. She pressed tenderly.

"Wynn. This rubdown . . ."

"Hold still."

"I'm not moving a muscle."

"You've spread your legs too far apart."

Elsa glanced down. Her heels rested on opposite sides of the bed. When had she done that?

"I can't do your other leg as well when you move it so far away."

Elsa drew her legs together. Involuntarily, she arched her back, thrusting her pelvis upward. "I want you to massage my whole body, Wynn. Would it be all right? I mean, it wouldn't be wrong or anything, would it? It just seems that I'd feel better if you did." She was breathing hard and deep, each breath a sharp pain.

"You'd better relax, sweetie. You're gonna hurt something."

Sweetie. Wynn called her sweetie. "I'll relax. I can relax. I'd like to get the best care I can so's I can get up for work tomorrow. I know I'll be better if I'd just calm myself once in a while. I never calm myself. I'm always nervous and jumpy. I'll calm myself."

"You jump once and I stop."

Without a qualm, Elsa allowed Wynn to fully disrobe her as their gazes locked and their breathing deepened and increased. Unclad, Elsa lay still as she watched Wynn's hands move an inch or two, lingering on this area and then lingering on that area. Wynn slid her hands to Elsa's feet, flexing her fingers and working upward toward Elsa's knees. Her hands slipped behind them, rhythmically compressing the tightened tendons.

Elsa concentrated solidly on remaining still. It was becoming nearly impossible. "You sure know how to do this well. The horses must love it."

"I don't do this to horses."

"Why not? It's grand."

"It's not necessary."

Wynn's hands were on top of Elsa's thighs rubbing, rubbing, rubbing.

"I need to move a little, Wynn."

"Go ahead."

Elsa couldn't help herself. She *had* to spread her legs. Just a little. It was *necessary*. "There, that's more comfortable." She opened her eyes.

Wynn was staring at her, not at her eyes, but down there! Her mouth was opened, and she was panting deeply, too.

"Are you getting tired?" Elsa asked in a throaty whisper. "We can stop."

"No, no, I'm fine. Just a little thoughtful. I can keep going." She'd gamble she'd like it.

Gamble. All the wonderful emotion building within her body and mind began draining out of her like sand through an hourglass. She fought to hang onto her sense of amour, recalling visions of sunshine and sounds of comforting rain pattering on the roof as she read by the attic window. She recalled the wonderful times she rode the bay and conversations she'd had with the horse. The word *gambling* slipped from her mind.

"You're not with me," Wynn said. "Had enough?"

"I'm fine. Just a little twinge in my head. It's gone now." Elsa focused on the room, on Wynn's healing therapy and strong leathery hands.

"If you're not, you tell me. I wouldn't hurt you for the world, sweetie."

There was that "sweetie" again.

Wynn placed her hand between Elsa's legs. "This okay?"

Blood rushed through Elsa. She nodded, unable to speak.

Wynn's hand remained unmoving, and Elsa was able to collect herself somewhat. Then the hand moved again, and the fingers. "Where?" Wynn asked.

Elsa opened her eyes. Wynn was sitting as rigid as a park statue. She looked a bit wild-eyed, yet her touch remained sensitive to Elsa's vulnerable nerves. "Could you move up a little closer?"

Wynn shifted, her hip pressing against Elsa's breast. How comforting. How caring it felt. "I like your rubdowns, Wynn. They're perfect. Maybe you should become a nurse."

"I'll be your nurse."

Wynn moved her hand in a circular pattern, pressing against Elsa and all those folds of skin that Elsa knew were down there. The whole sight of that area seemed overly designed the last time Elsa had studied it, which she did from time to time while wondering why there were so many flaps of skin. They didn't *do* anything. Until now.

"I never felt like this before."

Wynn chuckled. "Oldest line in the book."

"What book?" Elsa whispered. She couldn't think about books. A new sensation was welling up within her where Wynn was touching her. It blocked out anything going on around her, any thought, any deed. The house could fall down on them and she wouldn't have cared. She probably wouldn't have known.

She cried out something incoherent and slammed her hand down on top of Wynn's. Breathing was torturous, lying still, impossible. Her hips refused to stop pumping up and down. Her moans continued. Her heart was going to burst.

"Wynn," she gasped. "Wynn." She pressed Wynn's hand against her. Her zenith reached, she drifted back to the bed. "Wynn."

Wynn withdrew her hand. She lay beside Elsa and held her gently. Strands of loose hair clung to Elsa's damp forehead. Wynn carefully brushed them aside and rested her forehead against Elsa's cheek.

"Lucky horses." Elsa experienced her first sensation of jealously.

"This is a special treatment, meant only for you."

Elsa could not quite comprehend why she was selected. It felt good to be chosen as someone special for something, boring and drab as she was. But Wynn didn't seem to think so.

Wynn rested on one elbow. She ran her fingers along Elsa's jawbone. "You could give massages like this."

"Not me!"

"You'd pick who to give them to. It wouldn't be just anybody."

"If it was anybody, it'd be just you."

Wynn looked deeply into Elsa's eyes. "Do you tell lies?"

Elsa returned Wynn's stare. "Only lately and only because I had to."

"Are you lying now? Would it be only me? Would I be the special person?"

Elsa thought about marrying. Why would she have to if she and Wynn could rely on each other all the time? "I'm not lying. You'd be the special person. Always."

Wynn snuggled in Elsa's arms. "This feels great."

Elsa thought so. Were it not for her aches and

pains, notably relieved and then revived from Wynn's vigorous massage, she'd feel perfect.

Perhaps even pretty.

"You're independent, aren't you?" Wynn asked as she lay comfortably in Elsa's arms.

Elsa shut her eyes, treasuring Wynn's closeness. "I'd like to think so." But it wasn't true at all, unless she counted stealing money or fighting with her mother all over the kitchen for a few coins to get herself here.

"I like independent women," Wynn said.

Ten more seconds and Elsa would be asleep. "I'd better go. Mama will worry."

"Mamas are like that." Wynn dressed Elsa using the same care, Elsa giggling and blushing and helping, too.

"How'd you get into show business?" Elsa asked. She relied heavily on Wynn to get her on her feet.

"My parents have a cattle ranch in California. That's where I learned to ride. It about killed my mother when I told her I wanted to join Cody's show. She did everything to stop me except shoot me, but I came anyway."

"Did your father want to shoot you, too?"

"Not Dad. The first time he ever saw my mother was when he stopped at the Canyon Ranchero. She was out in a corral busting horses."

"She was?"

"The men were all out on roundup. It's a hard life."

It sure was. But so were Papa's debts and the threats hanging forever like an ominous black storm over her and Mama.

CHAPTER TEN

Elsa returned home, her head so crammed with emotions and memories that she couldn't dwell upon a single one. Wynn chose her to be her special person. Elsa could make a fortune riding broncos. Wynn made her feel like never before. Papa's debt would no longer be a burden to Mama and her. At twenty-five dollars a win she would soon be free. From head to toe, her body cascaded with pain. She could pose as a young man and hire herself onto a ranch. She had left Wynn only ten minutes ago and already she missed her.

The omnibus stopped before her house, releasing her from her jumbled musings. Walking at her usual pace and swinging her arms at their normal rate, she went inside. Mama waited for her.

"You're pretty late, missy." Knitting needles rapidly clicked as the formation of a stocking took shape.

"The show was longer than I thought, Mama. I'm sorry."

"You'll be sorrier when you get up in the morning dragging around like a half-dead alley cat."

In an unusual move, Elsa bent and kissed her mother's cheek. "You're right, Mama. But I promise not to complain." Even if she needed to scream in pain, she would smile instead and go about her business as though she wasn't feeling like a vise was torturously squeezing her flat between its mighty iron jaws.

Visibly surprised by the gesture, her mother's sharp scolding softened. "Breakfast will be ready on time."

" 'Night, Mama. Go to bed yourself. This light is no good to knit by." The lamp burned with a frugal flame, conserving whale oil against the time when it might truly be needed.

Elsa slept fitfully, dreaming about the screaming crowd and being tossed about like a rag doll on a bronco. The nightmares were so real that she moaned in her sleep. She attempted a number of times to wake herself up, but movement was so arduous she gave up, surrendering to her miserable dreams and distress. In the morning, Mama called her to breakfast.

Elsa opened her eyes, her lids swollen with sleep.

Cheerily she called out, "Be right there," feeling not at all cheery, but more like she'd been trampled by the horse she'd ridden all night long.

She dressed, gritting her teeth, each move a reward of agony.

She ate breakfast, chatted, put on her hat, grabbed her lunch and walked to work as though today were like any other. She wished it were yesterday once more. She wished she didn't have to go to work — ever again. A thought briefly flickered but died before she could grab onto whatever it had been.

At work she continued her falsehood, smiling at customers, talking happily to any who spoke with her, pretending all was well. She glanced at the store's large wall clock. It was rapidly approaching noon. She must return the money before she went to lunch.

As before, she checked the floor walker. Right on schedule, he was at the furthest reaches of the store. She had only to open the cash drawer and return what she had stolen yesterday. It would take seconds, and then she would be released and relieved of the awful, evil thing she had done.

Casually she walked to the cash register. She had been unable to leave the drawer ajar as she had before. No clients had come near lingerie for the last half-hour. Having no choice, she pushed the No Sale button, sounding the register's bell. Without hesitating, she rammed the money into the drawer and snapped it shut.

"What do you think you're doing?" Miss Ashley was right behind her. How much had she witnessed? Elsa must do what Papa had done all his life: bluff.

"I beg your pardon?" Her heart pounded, her ribs throbbed, yet she faced her supervisor calmly.

"I asked you what you're doing. And don't get uppity with me, Elsa."

"I'm sorry." She hung her head as she always had when she was scared or unhappy or embarrassed. She'd hung her head most of her life.

"Look at me when I'm talking to you."

You're talking *at* me, Miss Ashley, she privately thought, and I *hate* it. She gazed directly into Miss Ashley's eyes. "I was making a cash check before going to lunch."

"A what?"

"A money count. I often do before I leave."

"I've never seen you do any such thing." Ashley looked so skeptical that Elsa battled not to blurt out the truth.

"Often." She remained firm. "Yesterday a couple of bills were stuck in the back. I found them this morning. They're included in today's count. That's why I check. It's happened before."

Ashley rudely elbowed Elsa aside and opened the drawer. Again the bell rang. "I'll count it. How much should there be in here right now?"

"Thirty . . ."

"Never mind! Write it down."

Elsa jotted down the figures she knew were there and waited. Ashley began counting, muttering, "I know precisely how much was put in this morning and how many sales you've made since then. They'd better match, Miss Elsa."

"They'll match, Miss Ashley."

"Be quiet! I'm counting!" Elsa's supervisor took several minutes to be sure, tallying the cash three different times, the totals remaining identical each time. "I checked last night. It was ten dollars and twenty-five cents short."

"Not when I left."

"You're lying." Ashley's beautiful face became hard, cruel and pitiless. She tallied the count once more. "All right," she said. "I don't know what's going on here, but I'll be watching you."

Wordlessly, Elsa went to lunch, sitting off by herself, dwelling upon her near misfortune. Other girls chattered happily nearby, but she wasn't listening. She had won! Against the clock and the horse last night and against Miss Ashley this noon. The intriguing flash she had earlier again ripped through her brain. She tried to grab onto it, but it was already gone.

The day turned out beautifully, the sun deliciously warming the air. Chickadees landed at her feet. She flipped them tiny bits from her sandwich, watching them scramble for the food.

She felt at peace, left only with a physical discomfort that seemed to increase since her mental anguish was now behind her. The theft had weighed more heavily upon her than her aching body ever could. That problem solved, she could savor her aches and bruises, knowing they were only temporary and nothing that could get her into trouble. She could control the pain, ignore it, bask in it.

She could also sit there in the sun with her eyes closed and think of Wynn and her hands. She could daydream about having won last night. She had so many choices. She thought she was quite a woman.

"Elsa!"

She leaped straight off the bench, her body rebelling all the way.

"Follow me." Miss Ashley was calling from the store's rear entrance. Elsa followed, clawing her way back to her senses through a haze of scorching, red pain as she ran to catch up with her.

Ashley strode into the company's main office. "Mr. Flowers would like a word with you."

"All right." Elsa smiled agreeably.

Flowers' office was wallpapered with a drab brown print that gave the room a shortened, squashed look. A large oak desk devoured most of its space with nothing on the highly polished surface save an inkwell, a desk blotter and an ashtray. Two expensively padded, brown leather chairs were placed in front of the desk. Flowers himself occupied another more costly seat behind the desk. Brass gaslights burned in spite of the light streaming in through a large window behind the desk. There was a four-drawer, oaken file cabinet and a thirsty-looking spider plant that hung from the ceiling. A large picture of the front of Flowers' Department Store hung conspicuously on the wall just to the right of the window.

Jeremy Flowers was a cadaverous-looking man. Behind small horn-rimmed glasses, sunken eyes rested in deep sockets. A stubble of beard colored his otherwise pale face. His neck was so thin the collar could not be drawn tight. His black suit, expensive yet ill-fitting, draped on his gangling frame. He smoked a long, thick cigar, the smoke coiling upward and filling the room with the stink of the burning tobacco.

He leaned forward, indicating that she should sit.

"Thank you." She smiled trying to sound as charming as possible as she obeyed him yet resisting a rising panic bubbling within her chest. Apparently the money question hadn't been settled after all.

"Miss Ashley has a question about you," he said in a deep, rumbling voice. "A most troubling one, I must say." Peering over his glasses, he closely scanned Elsa's face.

"Yes?"

"Did you or did you not steal money from the cash register yesterday, and did you or did you not return it today? I must warn you that returning it in no way exonerates you from a crime committed. Steps must be taken."

Her mind scrambled for an appropriate answer. Displaying wide, innocent eyes as terror gripped her heart and squeezed, she asked, "Is there something wrong with the count?"

Ashley moved next to her. "Just answer the question, Elsa." Elsa could smell her perfume, feel the heat radiating from her expensive green dress.

"You checked the drawer several times, Miss Ashley, and found nothing wrong with the count. You already know the answer."

"You are impertinent, young lady." Ashley's anger blanketed Elsa. She wished she dared stand and not have this dreadful woman hovering over her.

Flowers leaned forward, his piercing eyes exhorting an honest reply from her.

Elsa's hands were sweating badly. Traces of moisture collected on her forehead. She breathed deeply to calm herself. "I'm sorry, Mr. Flowers, that you've been given reason to doubt my integrity. I checked the cash yesterday at noon and checked it again before I left for the day. It was fine both times. Miss Ashley counted it ten minutes ago. She found the count correct as well."

"Are you in the habit, Miss Catulie, of checking the drawer's tally?"

"About twice a week or so," she said.

"It's not something I've told her to do, Mr. Flowers. Such a great deal of responsibility, you know. I've always kept track of my department's cash flow. It has never been incorrect until last night."

"Then why was I not informed last night?" he asked. The question hung in the air as he swiveled toward Ashley.

She shifted uneasily. "It seemed prudent to wait. I believed I might catch the culprit today. I certainly had my suspicions."

"It seems as though you may be mistaken."

"Yes, sir. I'll certainly increase my surveillance. You can be sure of that, Mr. Flowers." Ashley's gaze deliberately fell upon Elsa.

Elsa met Ashley's accusing look. Why, Miss Ashley's scared, she thought. She's afraid Mr. Flowers might think she's the one stealing the money.

Flowers stood, towering over Elsa in spite of the wide desk separating them. "All right, Miss Catulie, you may go."

Elsa was sure he had more questions. Papa, she thought as she left the office, I'm no better than you, and I'm learning a great deal about how your mind worked.

That evening, Mama sat on the davenport

mending a stack of laundry when Elsa got home. "I'll make supper tonight, Mama," she said. "Just let me rest a minute. It was real busy today."

"Thank you, Elsa. I could sure use your help."

Elsa gently lay down on the bed. She made herself as comfortable as possible and recalled last night and every detail of Wynn's massage, every stroke of her hand, every squeeze.

Her stomach spasmed. "I have to get *up*." She changed into a lighter housedress and went into the kitchen to prepare supper.

Later while washing dishes, the annoying thought that had skirted her consciousness earlier fully revealed itself, branding itself on the inside of her forehead and the backs of her eyeballs. Her hands stopped running the soapy rag over the plate. "Would it be possible?"

"Would what be possible?" Mama came in from the living room to help.

"Oh, nothing," Elsa said lightly. "Just a thought I had. My mindless dreaming again, that's all."

Mama picked up a plate and vigorously wiped it dry. She put it in the cupboard, saying, "I thought you were past that stage. Seems like lately you have been."

"I am, Mama. Once in a while I forget myself." But it was too late. The seed had been firmly planted.

That night in bed she lay immobile and still sore, contemplating the idea. Unable to find an opportunity to put her winnings in the money jar, they remained concealed in a shoe beneath her bed. That meant she could buy a ticket. That meant she could hire out as a bronco buster when the men were out on the range. That meant . . . quitting her job.

Her contemplating stopped short. She would *have* to succeed. If she rode the kind of horse she had last night, then she could ride anything. After awhile she shouldn't be so sore each time she rode. Maybe she'd get good enough to stop hurting altogether.

Her left leg cramped when she stretched in an effort to ease her discomfort. Grimacing, she grabbed her calf, rapidly squeezing the knotted muscle.

Eventually the spasm faded. She lay down again undeterred by her desire to ride broncos and get rid of Papa's debt as soon as possible.

"I want to go where I can break horses," Elsa blurted as soon as Wynn opened the door. It was only two days after the show. Wynn's jaw dropped in disbelief.

"I can make fast money. You said women make good money at the shows. I could do this out West. It'd be steady work."

Wynn's face remained frozen.

"What do you think?" Elsa closed the door and pulled Wynn to the davenport.

Wynn said slowly, "I've wondered how you've been. I don't think you're right in the head yet." She drew Elsa into her arms.

Elsa frowned and brushed aside Wynn's words, but not her arms. "I'm fine, Wynn. Listen. I could ride five broncos a day. That's a hundred and twenty-five dollars. That's six hundred, twenty-five dollars in a single week. I could make thousands in no time flat." Moving from Wynn's arms, she slid to the seat's edge, anchoring her elbows to her knees. Her hands cut the air in excited slashes.

Wynn reached for her again. "Elsa, sweetie, let me tell you the facts of life."

"*Now?*"

"Not those facts. Other ones."

"Not now. I want to talk about my idea."

Wynn took Elsa's hands in her own. "Things have a way of happening, and you're in the wrong place at the wrong time and your number comes up."

"I wouldn't make mistakes."

"All right, Mrs. God, tell me how you'll avoid them. I'll bet you could barely move these past two days."

"No one knew."

"Bull. You could hardly walk when you left here." Wynn released Elsa's hands. She crossed her arms in front of her and leaned back.

"You don't need to curse at me. And I didn't let on to anyone." Elsa smiled at her success. "I'm thinking about quitting my job and leaving for the western ranches."

"Are you kidding?"

"We'd have a good time."

"I'd bring you back here in a pine box. Unfinished wood."

"There's money to be made." Elsa looked obliquely at Wynn, feeling full of disobedience, yet smiling.

"Five dollars a ride out there, Elsa. Maybe seven."

"That's all?"

"That's it."

"Then I'll ride more horses. I can still do it."

"You'll die."

"I'll live. Who cares anyway? If I don't make the money, I'll still die." She slapped a hand over her mouth. "Just joking." She laughed.

"Why," Wynn asked slowly, "would you die if you don't make money?" She cocked her head, waiting for the answer.

"I was joking, I'm telling you."

Wynn got up and sat on Elsa's lap.

Elsa laughed happily, pulling Wynn against her while ignoring the ache of Wynn's weight on her legs. Together, the women collapsed backward against the davenport.

Wynn's sudden nearness set off heatwaves in Elsa's stomach and — lower. Her thighs weren't doing much better, but it wasn't an unpleasant occurrence.

Wynn laid her face along Elsa's cheek, her hair tickling Elsa's nose. She talked against Elsa's cheek. "You don't know how to ride, Elsa. Not broncos."

Elsa pulled back, rolling her eyes. "Never mind that now. Let's just enjoy the evening." Unconsciously, she cradled the back of Wynn's head and stroked the long soft tresses. "Oh." She drew back her hand as though she had placed it on Mama's hot stove. "I . . . I'm sorry. I wasn't thinking . . ."

Wynn nestled closer. "It's fine. Go ahead. It feels like a nice rubdown."

Shyly, Elsa returned to caressing Wynn's hair. "My, it feels silky."

"Cornmeal. Makes it softer. Something my mother taught me. Takes out a lot of oil. I use it every day."

"Feels nice."

"I just brush it out real well. It works. Makes me feel cleaner through the week until I wash it again."

"I need to get that money, Wynn," Elsa said, her brow furrowed in deep thought.

Wynn shifted in Elsa's lap. "Why? What can possibly be so bad that you'd willingly risk your neck at five dollars a ride?"

"Maybe seven."

"Okay, maybe seven." Wynn gripped Elsa's face between her hands. "Are you in trouble?"

"No." Not as long as she and Mama kept up their payments.

"Then why do you need so much money? Why won't you tell me?"

"You can't help. Only I can. And Mama."

"Mama, again."

"It isn't her fault, or mine."

"Then dump the problem. It's not yours."

"It . . . became ours. There are men that Papa owed money to. They told Mama to pay the loan . . . or else."

"Else?"

"We'd be in big trouble, Wynn. Big trouble. I want to pay them off as fast as I can."

"You could get killed in the process."

"I won't. I refuse to."

Wynn removed herself from Elsa's lap. She paced the room for several minutes, Elsa watching her. Wynn knew the West, knew ranching. If it could be done, then Wynn could help her. If not, she was stuck.

Wynn paused before the window. She pulled aside the worn, faded lace curtain and looked out at the dark street. "You have no idea how much I hate to sew, Elsa. I used to ride and now I sew and wash and iron. I hate it, Elsa. I hate it."

Wynn's back stiffened. Elsa longed to run to her, but something warned her away.

Wynn turned and faced her. "If I stay here, I'll wither up just like my arm and die. If I go, I can die watching the wild ponies. Not like the ones here," she said sadly. "Broken down old bags of bones pulling milk wagons and beer wagons that're too damned heavy for them. Half of them don't even get enough to eat. I feel sorry for these horses, Elsa. Sometimes I cry when they go clopping by. They should be out on the range, free to run and roll in the grass. I'm just like them, the city horses. But I know what life can be. I lived like that once."

She sat back down, her eyes filled with unfathomable agony. As she spoke, her suffering seemed to drain away, replaced by an inner light that Elsa had seen a long time ago, the night she first met Wynn. Then, Wynn was unbroken. Then, Wynn was a wild horse.

Wynn grasped Elsa's hands and raised them to her lips. Her warm breath was like the stroke of a feather as she spoke with quiet, tranquil stubbornness. "I'll go because I hate it here. I'll go just to go. And I'll go because you want to and to keep you alive, if nothing else. Now, let's see how much money we have between the two of us."

If either of them had been a man, Elsa would have kissed her right on the mouth.

CHAPTER ELEVEN

The sun hung suspended between earth and sky. The two women had ridden the train from New York City to Wawtauk, South Dakota, a growing town of cattlemen, miners and loggers. The trip had been long, tiring and frightening. Changing trains had taxed Elsa's patience and Wynn's strength. At third class rates, sleeping quarters were nil. People slept on each others' shoulders, in the aisles, curled in laps.

The saving grace of the interminable trip was the beauty of their new home as they drew closer and closer to their final destination. Elsa and Wynn repeatedly grabbed each other in their excitement to point out the vast rolling flow of the grasslands erupting in a jagged row of sawtooth peaks, entrance to the Badlands where genuine outlaws lived in spite of little water or grass.

The train jolted rocking the cars, their wheels screaming and sliding along the tracks. Unexpectedly it stopped.

"What is it?" Elsa asked in a nervous voice. The car's windows were already packed with faces straining to see what the problem was.

Several mounted horsemen, their faces concealed by bandannas, galloped by on both sides of the train. Elsa choked down rising fear. "Bandits," she whispered.

Wynn grabbed her hand. Men, most farm immigrants and unequipped to deal with gunmen, were already moving into position to protect their women and children, but few had guns.

"Let's just sit and wait," Wynn suggested. "We haven't got anything they'd want."

Other women had sat back down, pulling their children onto their laps and closer to their sides.

"Don't move, anybody!" A masked man entered the car holding a gun. "Drop your guns and I won't shoot." He swiveled his weapon toward a woman holding a baby.

Three guns were pointed at him. One by one, Elsa listened to them fall to the floor.

Wynn continued clutching Elsa's hand. "Don't talk. Don't whisper."

Elsa swallowed watching the outlaw move down

the aisle demanding money and jewelry. He held out a flour sack. Without arguing people dropped in their valuables.

Wordlessly he stopped by Elsa and Wynn.

"We haven't got anything," Wynn said.

He waited, the bag outstretched.

"We don't," Elsa added timidly.

He bent and pulled a carpetbag from beneath their feet. His eyes and his gun barrel never left their faces.

Elsa started to say something, and Wynn rammed her elbow painfully into her side.

The man gave Wynn a quick glance, then moved on carrying their bag with him.

Elsa winced as Wynn gave her a withering look and squeezed her hand even tighter.

The bandit took the men's guns before leaving the rear of the car.

Everyone sat stone-still until the train began moving again. Bedlam set in as men rushed from car to car cursing and yelling and women and children stayed huddled in their seats. But nothing could be done right now. The outlaws were gone, already specks in the distance.

"Our clothing and money is gone," Elsa said.

"Not this." Wynn pulled fourteen dollars out of her shoe.

In relief, Elsa closed her eyes and wiped away tears. She would succeed out here. She would.

Another hour's travel brought them farther southwest. There loomed the Black Hills in the distance, close to Wawtauk — if a day's ride could be considered close. The mountains rose from heights of a few thousand to several thousand feet. Ponderosa pine blanketed the mountainsides. Above them, bare rock jutted unexpectedly through the trees. Gold lay buried in the hills; the surrounding plains fed scores of herds of cattle.

The entire area was staggering in its beauty and wealth. The young summer was still merciful to the earth, the soil moist, the land blanketed with green grasses and thousands of nameless flowers. In far distances, herds of antelope grazed undisturbed. In other areas, wild horses and cattle roamed, getting fat on the lush prairie grass.

Shaking, Wynn and Elsa exited the train at Wawtauk. Less than a week ago, Elsa had broken the news to Mama. She was still reeling from that encounter and had hardly been ready for the second and even more petrifying. Even so, the memory of their fight came flooding back.

"You're *what*?" Mama had screeched.

Elsa remained in the living room and announced her intentions as Mama ironed in the kitchen. Eyes glaring, Mama came storming into the living room.

"I'm going out West with Wynn Carson to try to make better money," Elsa repeated. Yelling was no longer necessary. Mama stood not two feet from her.

"You're *crazy*."

"We leave tomorrow."

"You leave and where am I supposed to get the extra money you've been giving me, young lady? Just tell me that."

Mama's face was so red that Elsa thought she might faint, or worse, drop dead at her feet. Papa falling dead beside her flashed through her thoughts. She rushed to reassure Mama. "I can get good work out there. I can work as a cook in a hotel. The pay is better, a lot better than what I get at Flowers'. I can do it, Mama. We can get out of debt a whole lot sooner."

"Over my dead body."

"Don't *say* that, Mama. We're going to be free and clear of these people in a couple of years. We can do it! *I* can do it. I've already bought my ticket."

Mama slumped to the davenport. "Oh, my God. You must have stolen the money. And you who can't even walk to work without thinking somebody's going to kill you. How do you think you'll raise enough courage to put even one foot on a train?" She ran her hands through her hair, loose and ready for fresh braids before bed.

"I don't know, Mama," Elsa replied honestly. "But I'll find it because I'll have to. And I didn't steal the money. I found it in the dirt." She gathered her mother in her arms. "I'll be scared to death, but I'm more scared that our debt isn't being paid faster. I need to go, Mama. I'll write. I'll send word as soon as I get there. I'll need some of Papa's clothes."

"*What?*"

"Papa's clothes. I'll need a few things."

Mama really hit the ceiling then, but Elsa convinced her that with as few dresses as she had, she might have to wear Papa's workpants and boots. But she wouldn't unless she was in rags. She was a lady.

"You're a moron, that's what you are," Mama exclaimed.

The argument had ended there, and Elsa went

West with a few of Papa's clothes, thinking Mama might be half right.

As she stood in Wawtauk, she was convinced that Mama was more than half right. She needed to telegram her mother right away that she'd arrived safely.

They grabbed their one remaining bag and left the station. Wawtauk was unsettling. All her life, Elsa had been surrounded by closely packed buildings: tall and short, large and tiny, brick, stone and wood. Here the buildings were close enough together, and the single street in town was long enough with probably twenty-five assorted buildings on each side of the road, but the highest structure was only two stories tall, and every building was constructed of wood and in need of a good coat of paint. There were a few large tents squeezed between buildings. These, too, were part of the town, part of the business section.

Folks walked the boardwalks, entering and leaving various businesses. Elsa noted several saloons, a couple of cafés, an emporium, three hotels, a blacksmith's shop, a barbershop, even an opera house. The opera was housed in one of the tents, its frugal look well outshone by the gaudy overhead sign boasting that the best Shakespearian plays were produced there. And yet, for all Wawtauk's bustle, all the people in town didn't total enough to populate West Front Street.

"Slow down, will you?" Wynn complained. "We don't even know where we're . . ."

Two oncoming horsemen stopped them cold. One was tall and thin, his disheveled beard looking as though it might be full of live things. Covering his equally filthy long hair was perched a battered black hat with a large chunk torn out of the brim and two small, round holes piercing the crown. He wore a faded, tattered checked shirt tucked into black pants held up by greasy suspenders. Both knees were ripped open. One boot had lost its heel and both, most of their tan coloring. A wide, black gunbelt holstering a pearlhandled pistol rode low on his hip.

The second horseman wasn't sitting up. He was slung like a sack of coal across the saddle, securely tied in place with a rope. His hatless head hung at a strange angle. His face and hands were devoid of color.

"I'm gonna be sick," Wynn said.

"Don't look," Elsa said sensibly.

But they continued to stare. So did a number of men, women and children, who had gathered in the street.

"Shot in the back," said a grizzled old-timer who had stepped up to the corpse after the rough-looking cowboy entered the sheriff's office.

"He was a killer, Tom. You know it." An edge to her voice, a tiny woman whose face was concealed by a sunbonnet spoke to the old man.

"Don't matter. Never shoot a man in the back."

"Pfff. Men." The tiny woman stalked off. Several other women followed, and so did the children at sharp commands from their mothers.

Elsa was aghast, thinking again of her father falling to his knees, her gaze remaining riveted upon the corpse.

"Come, we'll leave this terrible place right now." Wynn took Elsa's elbow to steer her away from the scene.

Before Elsa could move, the cowboy exited the sheriff's office. He stopped at the edge of the boardwalk. Sheriff Deston, a tall, bearded man, stepped around him and checked the dead man's face against a wanted poster he carried. "It's him," he said, and handed the cowboy a slip of paper which he tucked into his shirt pocket.

The man stepped off the walk, his heelless boot making him tilt rhythmically up and down, up and down. Stoically he moved to his gruesome baggage and released the ropes so that the lifeless form slid to the ground in a stiffened heap. Deston dropped the poster and grabbed hold of the victim's boots, dragging him onto the boardwalk. The man's head bounced with a sickening thump against the edge of the walk. His boots landed heavily when Deston dropped them.

Elsa gagged and Wynn said, "Let's get out of here. Neither one of us needs this." Wynn started to move, but the sight of the dead cowboy again morbidly drew Elsa's attention.

The slayer took the reins of the dead man's horse then mounted his own, behaving as though no one else were present. People silently parted, providing him a wide corridor.

He didn't ride far. Across the street from the jail was the Wawtauk Bank of South Dakota. He dismounted and casually slung the reins of both horses over the hitching rail. When the man disappeared inside, Wynn expected to hear guns going off and see another dead man come rolling out the door.

Nothing of the kind happened and those left watching wandered off. "Blood money," said a corpulent man to others walking with him. His listeners nodded their assent.

Wynn and Elsa had barely moved ten yards toward the hotel before the cowboy emerged from the bank. This time he carried a fat white envelope, eyeballing all those he could see. He rode over to the emporium and went inside.

The two women watched to see what would happen next. Nothing did. "Let's go," Wynn said. "We've wasted enough time here." She had to drag Elsa along with her to keep her moving. "What *is* your fascination with that fellow?"

"Nothing," she answered, "except the envelope he has."

"You heard what that old man said. Blood money. We've got fourteen honest dollars. We can last through the night and more. Tomorrow we'll find out where the ranches are around here."

"Papa's pants were in the carpetbag. I need new pants."

Wynn closed her eyes. "We better plan something different. We can sleep and eat. We can't buy clothes. Not on fourteen dollars."

They walked toward the Wawtauk Hotel. "Rooms can't be more than a dollar a night."

"We have to eat."

Wynn stopped. Deep in thought, she gazed toward the Black Hills in the distance. "Take off your hat."

"I will not!" Elsa looked indignant. "I always wear my hat."

Wynn reached up and yanked it from her head. "Ouch, Wynn, that hurt." A hatpin fell to the board-walk. Elsa quickly retrieved it.

"Here, hold it just like this and smile like hell."

"Stop cursing." Elsa grabbed her hat and held it as Wynn had demonstrated: upside down.

"Now smile." Wynn's face crinkled in merriment. "Smile!" she hissed through clenched teeth. She began singing "I Dream of Jeanie with the Light Brown Hair." When she had finished, she said, "Cowboys sing all kinds of songs to cattle at night. I'm glad I learned a lot of them."

"It's lovely."

Wynn crooned two more melodies before a rangehand with jingling spurs walked by. As he did, he dropped a coin into Elsa's hat. Wynn nodded as she sang while Elsa stared at the man as he moved on down the walk.

"Smile," Wynn coached in between breaths.

Elsa smiled and studied the coin lying in the crown of her hat.

When Wynn finished her song, Elsa asked, "Do you know any songs about dead people?"

Wynn moved closer to Elsa. "You must forget what we've seen. It's a terrible thing that children and women have to witness that kind of wickedness in men, and that you saw your own daddy die. But please try to put it out of your mind."

"But if you sang over there by that poor, departed soul lying dead on the walk with not even a sister or a mother to mourn him, we might make better money."

Wynn stepped back, her brows drawn together. "Those books you read. You shouldn't read them."

"Why not?"

"They're not real, Elsa. Life isn't like you say it is in those books."

"Let's try. We can at least try, can't we?"

"I don't relish the idea of standing there singing next to a corpse filled with bullet holes and him looking pale as butchered beef."

"But he may have no family. Look at him just lying there like an old dead dog."

"He is an old dead dog," Wynn growled. "He killed people. That's why he looks like that now."

Elsa went back to stand by the deceased. She held out her hat and began singing a lamenting tune about a cowboy gone wrong and a family who missed him. Flat notes and rhymeless lyrics were enough to bring Wynn to her side.

"Just hold the hat," she said.

Elsa looked appropriately sad as Wynn intoned several songs about the poor dead boy. A number of people gathered to listen, and Elsa collected a few more coins.

An hour later, Wynn stopped singing. "I'm going. This body stinks, and the flies are driving me crazy."

They crossed the street and in the shadow of a store counted their money. Wynn hefted the coins in her hand. "It'd probably be cheaper staying at that room and board over there." She pointed to a large two-story clapboard house several yards down from the main street. "I don't know if I have enough songs in me to get more money. It'd take some time. Why don't you write me some ditties? I can make up the tunes."

The boarding house was run by a tiny, round, apple-cheeked woman with a contagious smile. Her graying coiffure was heaped haphazardly upon her head and held in place with numerous hairpins sticking halfway out. Her Irish accent had dulled some since she had moved here seven years ago and started this business, but her inflection was still lilting and musical. She wore a light, short-sleeved gingham dress protected by a print bib apron. Her arms were heavily freckled. As plump as she was, muscular strength showed through.

The house was clean with a large dining room, a reading room and kitchen downstairs. Six bedrooms were located upstairs, each plainly furnished with a double bed, one straight-backed, caned chair and a small bureau with mirror. On the bureau was a bowl and pitcher, and beneath the bed, a porcelain chamberpot. Beside the bed was a rag rug and on the bed itself, a thin mattress, cotton sheets and a down quilt.

Elsa and Wynn took a room with meals for two nights. Sitting on the edge of the bed, Elsa said, "I've made a terrible mistake, Wynn. I don't know who I thought I was. One of those silly girls in those books." She burst into tears.

Wynn rushed to her side and held her. "Never mind, sweetie. We'll go back home and between you, your mother and me, we can wash and iron and sew and make a real business out of it. We could do well if we really try."

"Mama warned me." Elsa wiped her nose with a hanky. "I'm sorry. I'm such a foolish dreamer. Mama's always mad at me about it. But it looked so easy in the books. And I lived through the bronco ride."

"Why don't you let me give you a rubdown? You'll feel better."

Elsa stopped sobbing immediately. "Yes, that'd be good. How about you? I could give one to you, too."

They lay side by side, Elsa face down. For days

they'd been sitting upright on the train. It was a blessing to stretch out alongside Wynn. It was heavenly just to stretch out. Wynn draped her arm across Elsa's back. Elsa had already moved into position.

Wynn propped herself on one elbow. Slowly she kneaded Elsa's neck and shoulders. Her palm flat, she drew her hand up and down Elsa's spine. "You feel very nice," she said.

"Mm."

Elsa allowed Wynn to work on her back and neck a few more minutes before suggesting she do the same to Wynn. "It's about time I learned how to do this," she said, struggling to sit upright, slowed by the sticky hot evening, her confining dress and the soothing feelings with which Wynn left her.

"Good idea. I haven't had a body-rub since leaving the show."

Elsa straddled Wynn's back, resting lightly on Wynn's rump. She brushed aside damp hair clinging to Wynn's neck. "You're hot," Elsa said.

"Blow on my neck," Wynn mumbled into the pillow.

Elsa leaned forward and softly blew. "Feels like goose down falling on me," Wynn said. She arched slightly, pushing against Elsa's bottom.

"Whoa, horse," Elsa said. She drew away from Wynn.

Wynn sank back to the mattress. "It's okay to sit on me. You're not that heavy."

Elsa hesitated, then resettled herself while continuing to knead Wynn's back and neck. "You feel just like a rock."

"My shoulders ... my arms," Wynn said. She

tossed aside the pillow and stretched her arms above her head.

Elsa had grown used to seeing the severe depression in Wynn's arm. It had been a nasty break set by somebody apparently no better than an apprenticed blacksmith, but over time, Wynn would become stronger, Elsa knew, as she once again absorbed her western heritage's inherent strengths and determinations. She would reclaim her soul out here. She hadn't been willing to go as far as California. South Dakota was west enough and suited her fine. There were cattle here, too. Her choice had satisfied Elsa.

Elsa's fingers lingered on the improperly healed break. She started over again, massaging Wynn from shoulders downward, almost lying atop of her each time she reached for the backs of Wynn hands, palms and fingers. Heat between them increased and receded like the Hudson's tide. There seemed to be an intense amount of warmth where Elsa's buttocks came in contact with Wynn's.

Wynn breathed shallowly, steadily and slowly exhaled. Occasionally, Elsa felt Wynn's hips elevate slightly, creating within Elsa sensations akin to fire and brimstone. But heavenly.

Wynn flinched in surprise when Elsa's hands slid to her ribcage.

"You want your sides done?" Elsa's breasts pressed delectably against Wynn's back.

"Sure." Wynn clamped her jaw shut while Elsa's hands roamed.

"This would feel better without all this cloth between us," Elsa said. But the clothes stayed on.

Elsa's fingertips were now sliding an inch beneath

Wynn's breasts and then, beyond. She caressed Wynn's nipples several times, whether purposely or accidentally, she couldn't be sure. It created startling disturbances deep within her belly, tumultuous palpitations spiraling downward and radiating to her centermost spot.

She arched and leaned forward, pressing heavily against Wynn's back. Her arms slid all the way around Wynn, her hands cupping her breasts. The delicate soft flesh molded perfectly to Elsa's hand.

Helplessly, Wynn rhythmically drove her hips into the sparse mattress. "Elsa," she repeated over and over, hammering the bed in fierce bucking motions. "Elsa."

Eventually, the palpitations and the heat within Wynn seemed to slacken. "Turn me over," she whispered.

Elsa moved aside and Wynn rolled onto her back. "I want to stare right into your eyes and dive into their deep blue, maybe even grab a fleck or two of gold from those irises."

Elsa caressed her cheek. "I didn't know if you'd like your bosom included or not, but it seemed like I should." She could feel hot moisture through her clothes. She wondered if Wynn was aware of her fervor, for that's certainly what it was. A huge, powerful lot of it, too.

"You should include my bosom."

Elsa arched slightly as Wynn threw a leg across Elsa's hips and compressed herself against her. "I'll have to have you try mine sometime. Not now, though. I'm really feeling relaxed right now." Her motions increased and then increased again. Her body rammed against Wynn's in steady rhythm. She breathed like she'd run a hundred miles without rest. She arched upward when Wynn squeezed against her and pulled back slightly when Wynn did.

"This is grand," Elsa said. "Grand, gra —" Her words were chopped off as she threw her legs apart and tugged at Wynn until she was on top of her, hissing through her teeth. She continued rocking until she collapsed.

Wynn remained full length covering Elsa, holding her tight. They swayed together until Elsa lay motionless.

Sometime later, Elsa said, "It's getting pretty late. We ought to eat and then go to bed."

"If we do, then we'll have to let go of each other. I'd rather not do that right now."

"Me, either."

They slept throughout the night unmoving and still in their day clothes.

CHAPTER TWELVE

The following morning dawned blistering hot. Wynn and Elsa rose at ten. They moved sluggishly, pulling and tugging at their clothing, freshening up as much as possible.

"We look like we slept in these," Elsa said.

Wynn laughed and grabbed Elsa. She threw her on the bed and landed on top of her. "Another rubdown?"

"It's a thought." Elsa pushed her off. "But later."

"Should we look together or head in different

directions?" They planned to start hunting for jobs immediately after breakfast.

"We should split up. Better chance maybe."

By three that afternoon, they had had no luck. Defeated, Wynn said, "I'll sing again."

This time they chose a busy corner by Zannie's Saloon. Elsa removed her hat and pasted on her smile. Wynn began with a haunting melody of a dying cowboy and his girlfriend's heart breaking in two. Three cowboys dropped coins in Elsa's hat before entering the saloon. A few people walking on the boardwalk and a couple of men from inside paused to listen. Several more coins clinked against those already collected.

From across the street, a clean-shaven, well-dressed man approached them. His moustache was freshly trimmed, his cheeks were soft and pink. His black shimmering hair had also been washed and cut.

Everything he wore appeared brand new and store-bought: pressed black pants, bright new plaid shirt, snappy orange suspenders. His tan vest was of the softest leather. He wore a brown ten-gallon hat, the headband made of rattlesnake skin, not yet sweat-stained. The man's boots had a fancy stitch decorating black and brown leather, and the boots' heels added another two inches to his six-foot frame. The only thing aged upon him was a well-worn gun belt.

He didn't pause as he headed for the saloon, but as he passed Elsa, he dropped in a coin. "Thank you, sir," she said, smiling gratefully. She glanced down to see what he had donated as the batwing doors came to a creaking halt behind him.

Elsa lurched, her smile changing to one of amazement. Just as quickly, she recovered herself and smiled again at the few people watching.

Wynn completed her song, then asked, "What'd he put in there, a snake?"

"Look." Elsa offered her hat. In it lay a ten-dollar gold piece.

Wynn stared for several seconds and then turned to look toward the batwing doors. "The man who brought in the dead fellow," she whispered.

Somberly, they drifted away from the door and returned to their room full of mixed thoughts about the gold piece. They studied it over and over, passing it back and forth between them. Elsa bit it to see if it would dent.

"Don't put that dirty thing in your mouth." Wynn snatched it from her.

"I wonder just how dirty it is," Elsa said. "I think it's reward money."

In the end they sang no more. They could not abide the possibility that the killing cowboy might drop additional money in Elsa's hat.

They were not comfortable with the coin, but having earned it honestly and knowing that the bounty hunter had done the same, no matter how horridly, they would use it for rent and meals and remain at the boarding house without worry for the next several days.

A couple of days later before either Elsa or Wynn had opened their eyes to the light of day, there came a sturdy knock upon their door. They released each other immediately, Elsa sensing there was something about holding Wynn that wouldn't sit well. The knock was repeated as Elsa yanked her dress over her head. "Who is it?" Wynn was dressed and pulling on her shoes.

"Mrs. Kettle."

"Oh, please, come in." Elsa secured her last button.

Mrs. Kettle waddled in, a tray in her hands. "Brought you coffee," she said. She handed each of them a well-appreciated thick white mug brimming with black coffee.

Wynn's eyes lit up. "What's the occasion?"

"Got a question for you. But I can't ask only one of you ladies."

"Please have a chair," Elsa said.

Mrs. Kettle settled herself while Wynn and Elsa sat on the bed, each cradling her cup between her hands.

"I've had lots of boarders come and go and none cleaner than you two. I haven't had to make your bed or dust or sweep this room."

"Well, it seems like we can help out a little . . ."

Mrs. Kettle put her up hands. "No, no. That's my job even when ladies live here, which isn't too often. Pleases me to have womenfolk about. Not too many of us around."

"I'd noticed that myself," Wynn said.

So had Elsa. She told Wynn that it made her a little nervous that there weren't more women and children in Wawtauk.

"I got an idea," Mrs. Kettle said to them, "that if the other rooms were kept as clean and neat as this one is, I'd have happier travelers here, both the overnight ones and the longer staying ones. The overnight ones would remember, and the stay-longer ones might stay longer. I can't always keep up with the cleaning like I want and the cooking, too. I gotta put three meals a day on the table and I'm only just making it. Some beds get made, some don't. Can't give 'em fresh water each morning. You look like strong girls, except for your bum arm there, Miss Carson, and your gimpy leg. But it don't seem to hamper you much. So how about it? One of you want a job? Steadier than singing to those damn drunks down at the saloon."

"Can you give us a minute to talk this over?" Elsa asked.

Wynn glanced at Elsa as though she were throwing money off a cliff. Smiling tightly, she said to Mrs. Kettle, "Won't take but just a minute."

"Of course, girls, I understand. Singing might be a lot more fun than feeding a bunch of trail hands eating like pigs. I'll be downstairs."

Her eyes never lost their sparkle as she left them to discuss their opportunity.

Once the door was closed, Wynn whirled on Elsa. "We *will* take the job, Elsa. We *need* it."

"Of course we'll take the job. The question is, which one of us."

"You will."

"I hate housecleaning. Always did."

"You can do it better. I can shovel horseshit better."

"Wynn!"

"I've lived in a barn. You've lived in a house. You clean, I can still sing."

"Not by yourself. What if that bounty hunter comes by?"

"I'll smile, take his money and sing on key. We need cash."

"You won't sing at all. How much is the pay here, anyway? Did either of us even think to ask?"

Wynn stalked over to the door. "I'll ask." She flung it open to shout her question down the stairs.

"Eighteen dollars a month and room and board." Mrs. Kettle stood right outside the door.

"Thank you," Wynn snapped and slammed the door in Mrs. Kettle's face. She could be heard chuckling as she descended the squeaking staircase. "Damn!"

"Never mind, Wynn," Elsa said. "She's probably lonely."

"She's nosey, that's what she is. Now, you take the job. It's a five-dollar raise for you. I can sing. I can't lift much weight with my arm yet."

Elsa said, "I'll agree only if you sing in the daytime where other women are likely to pass by."

"And by the saloons only between eleven and one."

Elsa pondered this a moment. "All right."

Wynn brought in enough each day to pay for her rent and food. Elsa washed bedding, cleaned rooms and helped in the kitchen.

One morning in their room, Wynn wrapped her arms around Elsa. "How good you feel, sweetie. How wonderful. I'm so glad we've decided to be special friends."

Elsa snuggled against her. "So am I, but I worry for Mama, and I worry for myself."

"Why don't you have your mother move out here

with us? She could escape those thieves then. They'd never find her here."

"I'd already thought of that and asked her to come with us, but Mama said they told her they'd follow her to California if they had to."

Wynn sighed deeply. "I'll bet they would, too."

Elsa released Wynn, saying, "I need to go to the mercantile for Mrs. Kettle. Want to walk with me?"

At nine a.m., Wawtauk was fully awake. Wagons rolled by. Cowboys stopped and dismounted entering the bank or the small café where the coffee was terrible but strong and the rolls hard but sustaining. At the south end of town, the ringing of a hammer could be heard shaping a cherry-red bar of metal to properly fit a hoof.

Elsa scanned the scenery before her, the stores lining the wide street, the spacious unbroken sky above, the now familiar sounds that filled the town at this hour: hawks circling high overhead, calling in the distance. At night she could hear the occasional howling of wolves or coyotes. "I like this place, Wynn. I'm so used to all that traffic back home. At first, I missed the noise and bustle, but not anymore. I never knew what peace was until I'd been here a week or two. Not counting our terrible start."

"I'd reach out and take your hand if I thought people wouldn't look at us funny," Wynn said quietly. "I feel the same way although I must admit that I miss all the cheering people when I rode . . ."

They were halfway across the road when a thunderous explosion split their eardrums and the front of the bank completely disintegrated. Glass, brick, stone and mortar ripped through the air as though shot from a heavy cannon. Then as suddenly as it had happened, the noise stopped. Two seconds passed before the clamor began again. This time it was people shouting, women crying hysterically, men shooting. Bullets flew everywhere and shoppers and store owners out to breathe the fresh air threw themselves to the ground, to the boardwalk, into the nearest opened door.

Horses raced by as Wynn and Elsa stood paralyzed, staring at where the front of the bank used to be. They hadn't thought to get down. They could see little, the air clouded with smoke, fire and dust.

"Look out!" Wynn shouted. Her warning came too late. Several horses thundered down upon them, their riders looking back over their shoulders, heedless of whatever might be in their path.

Wynn was struck on the cheek with a spur as a rider galloped by. She went down, cut. Pinned between two other riders, Elsa was knocked down and rolled in the dirt two or three times before she lay still, staring up at the sky.

Pursuing men scrambled to mount up, their horses fearfully whinnying and prancing while their riders cursed and yanked at their reins to settle them down. A woman sat near the bank, weeping quietly. A child lay nearby.

An elderly gentleman with watery blue eyes helped Elsa to sit up. "I'm fine," she assured him. "Just let me see how my friend is." On her feet, she swayed until she steadied herself, then went to Wynn.

"What happened?" Wynn asked. A woman cradled

her bleeding head in her lap. She struggled to rise as Elsa helped her to her feet. Several women milled around them. "Anybody hurt?"

"Two men killed, one gal cut by flying glass," the woman said. "That boy was knocked out. He's fine now." The child, indeed, was walking around.

"I was just talking about how much I liked this place," Elsa said shakily as they left for the boarding house.

"It's just the men, sweetie, and only the wayward ones at that. They're the ones tearing up the territory. Nobody else."

"You're darned forgiving." Elsa pressed her handkerchief against Wynn's cheek. She was still bleeding. The sight nauseated and enraged Elsa.

Within a few days the town had cautiously settled down, alert to any unusual noises or comings and goings of strangers. Hammering could be heard from dawn to dusk as a newer and more secure bank was constructed. Funerals had been held for the men killed in the blast.

Lives were back to normal except for the dark thoughts Elsa carried around in her head, thoughts that built one upon the other. Sometimes she believed she could crush a rock bare-handed, her rage grew so. And then she would calm down for a day or two before the demons took hold of her again.

They were walking to church one clear Sunday morning when a haggard-looking rider leading two corpse-laden horses rode past them. He pulled up before the jail and was in and out in minutes. Sheriff Deston checked the bodies draped across their horses and handed the rider a slip of paper. "You'll have to wait till morning," he said. "Bank opens at eight.

Leave your gun outside. Man posted there who'll hold it for you."

"Good enough."

The dead were released and let fall to the ground. The cowboy took away the extra horses. He wore the same clothing of another man, a cleaner man who had been dressed like a dandy the day he dropped a ten-dollar gold piece into Elsa's hat.

Unnoticed, a paper fell from the bounty hunter's back pocket. As Wynn started for church, Elsa put a restraining hand on her arm. "Wait, I want to see what it says." As soon as the rider's back was turned, Elsa hurried over and snatched up the paper. "Look," she said. Her eyes grew wide. "It's a poster of those two dead outlaws that man just brought in. And three more, too. And look at this." She pointed at a row of numbers beneath the men's pictures. "Five hundred dollars for each man brought in and *ten* thousand dollars for returning the bank's money."

Wynn whistled softly. "But I'd still like to catch them just for running us down."

CHAPTER THIRTEEN

Throughout the night, Elsa tossed and turned, thinking about the amount of money the manhunter would claim as soon as the bank opened. For two crooks, he was going to collect a thousand dollars. Elsa could barely imagine it. Were she a man, she'd go after the rest of them. That'd be one thousand, five hundred dollars for the three of them. And if she recovered the stolen money, there'd be another *ten* thousand. She rolled over impatiently.

"Would you *please* go to sleep, Elsa." Wynn moved

away from her where she had been nestling. "You're worse than that bronco you rode back home."

"Sorry," Elsa said, still thinking about the money. "But I could never bring them in dead."

Wynn sat up, her voice thick with sleep. "Are you dreaming, or what?"

"Dreaming."

"Then dream and don't talk. I'm tired."

Elsa settled down and rubbed Wynn's back. Not having been on horseback in so long, Wynn's muscles weren't quite as tight as they once were, but with the exception of her injury, her arms continued displaying well-defined muscles and strong veins running along their length. And her stomach still looked like a washboard. She was beautiful.

That was Elsa's final thought until the sun streaming through the opened window struck her in the face and woke her to a new day and its predictable, uneventful responsibilities.

Wynn slept on. Days later, the side of her face still carried a large, yellowish bruise. For a long time, she would have a scar from the cut she took by the spur. She moaned in her sleep.

"I *hate* those men," Elsa whispered passionately. "Don't worry, my special friend, they'll pay for this."

Storms raged within her with each pin she angrily shoved into place, securing her thick braids to her scalp. People had hurt her special friend.

"Hell," she said because she really wanted to curse, "Wynn's no special friend to me. I love her. Period. No getting by it. I love her, by darn." She had privately repeated that statement for a solid week, and it still made sense. "I'll fix them," she said. "I'll fix them." She ran to the wash bowl and threw up. Even thinking about fixing "them," whoever "them" was, scared her, the "them" here seemingly as deadly as the "them" back home.

Flopping on the bed, she wiped a film of sweat from her brow.

Wynn rolled over. "What's going on?"

Elsa took Wynn's hand. "Time for work."

"Oh." Wynn turned back. "Wake me in a while. We both have work to do."

Elsa finished dressing and left with the fouled washbasin. It was time to cook breakfast.

As usual, she and Mrs. Kettle prattled on about this and that, with a great deal of the conversation still centered around the two-week-old bank robbery. No new bodies had been brought in. No arrests made. The eighty thousand dollars was still missing.

"How's Wynn today?" Mrs. Kettle asked. From the butcher-block work table center of the kitchen, she picked up a tray laden with flapjacks, homefries, crisp slices of ham and bacon, and fried eggs, then whisked out the door.

On a large cookstove, Elsa continued flipping pancakes until Mrs. Kettle rfeturned, the empty tray tucked beneath her arm. She was beet-red from hustling, her hair tumbling into disarray strand by strand.

"She's sleeping," Elsa answered as though Mrs. Kettle had never left the room. She added another flapjack to the golden pile already burying two plates.

Mrs. Kettle transferred them to her tray, adding a pitcher of molasses and a quart jar of peach jam. "If I'd had a gun that day, I'd have shot every one of those devils." She disappeared again. As the door swung back and forth on squeaky hinges, Elsa listened to the boarders laughing boisterously and the clinking of silverware against plates.

She pictured Mrs. Kettle courageously standing in the middle of Main Street, brave as Mountain Kate, just daring the dangerous bank robbers to ride past her. Steadfast, unshaken, hand and eye steady, Mrs. Kettle would take careful aim with her pistol and singlehandedly shoot each bandit as he rode down on her. One by one they would tumble headlong from the saddle, mortally wounded at her feet, one on top of the other until there was nothing left except a mound of dead bodies.

"That's what I'd do," Mrs. Kettle said upon her return. She set the tray aside and momentarily rested on a three-legged stool. "They'll be needing more coffee and just a few more jacks in about three minutes."

"Coming up." Elsa wiped away stinging sweat pouring into her eyes. The day was going to boil blood before the sun went down.

"That should be enough." Mrs. Kettle hefted the final tray carrying it with two thick cloth pads. "You're a good cook, Elsa," she said over her shoulder. "I couldn't have hired a better one." Elsa blushed at the praise.

"You eat yet?" Wynn entered through the kitchen's side door.

Deadpan, Elsa looked into her eyes.

Wynn frowned. "How are you, today?" She came over and patted Elsa's shoulder. "Happy as ever, I see."

"Your face, your hurts. They make me mad."

"Me too. What's for breakfast?"

"Help yourself."

Wynn loaded her plate with ham, eggs, a slab of warm bread and three pancakes that Elsa had set aside for her. She poured molasses over it all.

"You're disgusting," Elsa said. She wiped away more sweat streaming into her eyes and down her cheeks. There was a large spot of moisture seeping through her blouse between her breasts. She could feel another band running the length of her back.

Nonplussed, Wynn stuffed her mouth full of a large piece of molasses-drenched egg. "Others have told me that."

Elsa began to clean up, scraping the excess batter from the bowl. "Where are you singing today?"

"I'm not and you're quitting your job."

Else looked up sharply. "You're batty." Her spoon scraped angrily and none too gently against the bowl. Mama and she banked on the predictability of her salary coming in, the way a train counted on a well-built trestle holding up each time it crossed the bridge. The lack of either could get somebody seriously hurt.

"We're going after those men, when announced."

The container slipped from Elsa's hands, landing with a clatter against the table's thick surface.

Mrs. Kettle came in, scowling fiercely. "What on earth is going on in here?" She tolerated absolutely no nonsense in her kitchen, her domain, her kingdom with its many pots and pans hanging overhead, spice racks built along one wall, stacks of dishes and silverware filling the shelves and the sink loaded with dishes indicating a busy woman, like a body should be. She looked ready to explode.

"I'm sorry, Mrs. Kettle." Elsa's voice shook as she

scraped the bowl. "No damage done. There was some batter on the outside. It slipped."

"Well, see that it doesn't happen again. Bowls don't grow on trees, you know."

"Yes, ma'am."

Mrs. Kettle set down a tray of empty plates and saucers, muttering things under her breath.

Wynn ate her scrambled eggs. "I hear Elsa's quitting her job, Mrs. Kettle." Her face was inches from her plate, her eyes downcast.

Elsa whirled. "I said no such thing, Mrs. Kettle. Wynn here seems rattled in the brain this morning. Making trouble, she is. Just making trouble."

Mrs. Kettle's eyes shifted from Elsa's to Wynn's to Elsa's.

"It's true," Wynn said. "Elsa told me this morning that she's so mad at those bank thieves, she's going to quit her job and go catch them."

"I said no such thing. You just shut your mouth, Wynn. I'm sorry, Mrs. Kettle. She doesn't know what she's saying."

Calmly, Wynn answered, "Yes, I do." She carried her plate to the sink and placed it in the dishpan. "Elsa has it all planned out and a darned good reason for going after those men."

Mrs. Kettle folded her arms and planted them firmly across her ample chest. "And just what might that be?"

"Money," Wynn answered. "There's good money in bringing in outlaws. And the stolen money, too."

"Don't listen to her, Mrs. Kettle." Elsa increased her speed of cleanup in an effort to prove to Mrs. Kettle how valuable she was to the boardinghouse and how hard she was working to keep her job. Only last week, Mrs. Kettle had overwhelmed her by giving her a one-dollar raise for being such a fine worker. Wynn was going to get her fired if she didn't close her mouth.

Mrs. Kettle's arms drew tighter, raising her breasts to new heights. She glared at Wynn. "You're addled, young woman. That knock in the head emptied your skull."

Pleasantly, Wynn replied, "Not at all, Mrs. Kettle. Not even a whit."

"You mean witless," Mrs. Kettle retorted. She left for more crockery.

Unasked, Wynn pitched in and washed dishes as Mrs. Kettle carried them in from the dining room. Wynn said to her, "Elsa was telling me only last night that she'd like to have all that money from capturing those men."

Mrs. Kettle paused. "And who wouldn't? That doesn't make it right. You're girls! Elsa, you get back to work."

Elsa was already working as hard and as fast as she could. "Yes, Mrs. Kettle. Don't you worry. I'll get Miss Carson straightened up."

At eleven, Elsa took a break before beginning the noonday meal. Wynn lay on the bed, her hands propped behind her head. "You still have this . . . this thought in your head, don't you?"

"Yep."

"Well, I don't want to tell you anything, Miss Carson, but I *am* a girl. I do girl kinds of things. I cook, sew, mend. Make beds. *Girl* things."

"Woman," Wynn corrected. "You're a woman. Once you hit sixteen, in some places as young as thirteen, you're considered a woman."

Not now, Elsa wasn't any woman. She was nothing but a little child, one so tiny that she couldn't go anywhere that posed a threat to her. Standing five feet, eight inches tall in no way made a woman of a girl. "I'm not leaving."

"Damn it, Elsa, would you look at us? We're struggling and getting nowhere. I used to have a lot, you know." Elsa knew. "But now I don't. I'm gimpy-legged. My right arm isn't so strong anymore. I'm missing *teeth,* Elsa, *teeth.* I had beautiful teeth once. And my arm and fingers."

"They're getting stronger, better. You don't limp so much either."

"Yeah, but I used to have money, a life, strength, looks, *Buttons,*" she cried out. "People cared about me. Who I was. What I did."

Elsa lay down beside Wynn who'd begun to weep into her pillow. "All right, my dear, dear friend. It's all right." She smoothed Wynn's hair and rubbed her chest and arms and stomach. At last she could listen with full understanding. She wasn't the only one suffering great loss. Wynn's losses were at least as enormous as hers, something she hadn't fully acknowledged before. Wynn's anguish seeped into the room and into Elsas soul. "My dear one," she whispered against Wynn's ear.

Wynn's sobs receded to quiet tears. She lay wrapped in Elsa's arms for a long time before speaking. She said, "Boots. I notice boots. Good boots kept me in the stirrups. That's what riders want more than anything else; good boots that'll keep their feet steady in the stirrups." She paused then continued. "One of those riders had the same boots as the ones on the train. He was the one that cut my cheek. Black leather, fancy stitching. It's the same damned bunch of skunks." Her voice dropped to a whisper. "I want to go after them, Elsa. This is twice now," she said rising on one elbow. "I don't like it, not one damned bit."

"That bounty hunter will get them. He's probably out chasing them right now."

"Maybe, maybe not. But what's to stop us from trying too, I'd like to know."

"In my case, fear."

"Oh, posh." Wynn sounded stronger, less defeated. "Who wouldn't be afraid? Those men shoot people. You think I wouldn't be afraid? The very thought scares me."

"Makes me throw up."

"So? Everybody's got some little stumbling block."

"Stumbling block? We're discussing an entire granite mountain here, Wynn. I know what I am. I'm a coward. Girls usually are, and I'm as girl as they get when it comes to being a coward."

Wynn breathed deeply, patiently, exhaling slowly. "You have to stop thinking that you're still a girl. We're women and we're brave. Remember riding that bronco to full time? That's brave. Crazy, but brave. Got that?"

"All right, I'm a woman. And *maybe* brave, but so what?"

Silence reigned throughout the room. Through the open bedroom window, Elsa heard a dog barking. Children played somewhere nearby, their high-pitched voices ringing in the air. Horses nickered, blew and neighed as cowboys rode by.

Wynn sat up and straddled Elsa, her hands resting on either side of Elsa's face. She smelled like the soap she'd used to wash with earlier that morning. She must have just chewed a piece of mint leaf, for her breath was sweet. She had freed her hair, and it dangled forward. She tucked it behind each ear, but it fell again. Elsa could smell the familiar odor of corn meal. My, Wynn, Elsa thought. You are a lovely woman. There's no girl lurking anywhere within you.

"We could do it, Elsa," Wynn said, looking down on her. "We could go after them. We're as brave as anybody, and we're special friends. We can do anything together."

Wynn lowered her face close to Elsa's. Her lips were smooth, well shaped, pink without the added color she once used during her shows. Elsa resisted reaching up to touch her own lips to see if they were as soft as Wynn's looked.

Minutes passed before Elsa said, "Wish we could. It sure would get Mama and me off the hook back home."

"Consider it." Wynn drew another inch closer.

"I think . . . Wynn . . . Could we talk about something else for just a second? Could we talk about those rubdowns we give each other?"

"Now? You want to talk about them now?"

"I do."

Wynn looked just a little impatient. "What about them?" She had drawn back, still straddling Elsa's hips.

"Did . . . you . . . ever . . . I mean, when other people gave you rubdowns when you were in the Wild West show, did you ever feel like maybe . . . you . . . I don't know."

"What?"

"Well, like you might want to be . . . kissed?"

"Kissed? Women gave me rubdowns. Do you mean kissed by a woman?"

"Yes, by a woman. Actually, this . . . woman."

Wynn looked at her. "I don't know. I suppose the thought's passed my mind a time or two, but since we're both women I guess I never took it too seriously."

"Well, look at us. We're doing everything else with each other. What makes us stop at kissing?"

Wynn looked thoughtfully out the window. "I don't know. I guess just because we are both women. Rubdowns . . ."

"We touch places you've never had rubbed before I did it, Wynn. You've told me that a bunch of times."

"Yeah, but, it just seemed like they're better rubdowns with those places. But I've never wanted anybody *else* rubbing me there. They didn't, either!" Wynn paused. "One of my friends told me her husband just loved to suck on her . . ."

Quizzically, Elsa cocked her head. "Her what?"

"Her . . . ah, nipples."

"Oh." Elsa recalled a similar longing weeks ago when Wynn had rubbed *around* her nipples. Since that time, she hadn't come near them, at least not *sucking* on them. And she and Wynn sure as hell hadn't ever kissed. She shrugged. "I suppose those things could be part of a rubdown."

"None that I ever heard of." Wynn sat up and brushed back her hair.

Elsa rested her hands on Wynn's rock-hard thighs. "I never heard of *women* going after outlaws before either. How come it's okay to chase dangerous men, and it's not okay to touch each other's . . . nipples . . . or to kiss? What's the difference?"

"One's . . . normal. One's not."

"And which one is normal?" Elsa grabbed Wynn by her shoulders. She'd been having dreams for the past several nights about kissing Wynn, ever since she decided that Wynn was no silly special friend. Wynn was someone she was in *love* with. She wanted to kiss her.

Wynn looked questioningly into Elsa's eyes. "I don't know. I really can't say." She sounded truly perplexed.

"Let's kiss. We can try it. I keep dreaming about it."

"I dream about our rubdowns."

"I've never been kissed by anybody," Elsa said thoughtfully. "Have you?"

"A couple of cowboys. There was a woman, you know, the one I told you about from England, who got married and went back. I had a dream about kissing her once. Boy, that was a powerful kiss. But dreams are usually silly anyway."

"You'd be the first person who ever kissed me, Wynn. Why won't you?"

"It's strange."

Elsa drew Wynn down. Her heart quickened as their hips came in contact. Wynn shifted so that she nestled between Elsa's thighs.

Elsa said, "You like it on top best, don't you?"

Wynn smiled. "Yes, I do. But being on the bottom is good, too. Makes me feel like I'm safe from the world."

"That's how I feel."

They lay one on top of the other for several

minutes, their heat and breathing increasing as they teased each other.

Wynn's mouth was next to Elsa's ear. "I could think about kissing you, Elsa. I haven't just because it's not part of something I know about. Like touching your nipples. I don't know that women do those things. But I don't see why we couldn't think about it. Do you?" she asked tentatively.

"We could think about it. I'd like to." This wasn't the old Elsa she remembered of herself. Her safety shell she'd carried all her living days was displaying a slight crack in its surface. She felt a surge of acceleration she rarely experienced. The crack in the shell was there, but she wasn't afraid.

It was time for her and Wynn to make some serious decisions.

CHAPTER FOURTEEN

Mrs. Kettle raged at Elsa's ungrateful behavior for a full ten minutes before she turned her back on her and dismissed her from the kitchen. Elsa returned to her room burdened with guilt heavy enough to drive her to her knees. Closing the door, she said to Wynn, "You'd better be right." She didn't speak to her again until they left for the blacksmith's shop a half-hour later.

"We'd like to rent a horse and buggy and enough grain for the horse for a week," Wynn said to the bullish, whiskered man.

On the way, Elsa had stopped at the telegraph office and faithfully wired Mama the last of her wages. There would be no more if they failed to bring in the thieves, and she was certain Mrs. Kettle wouldn't take her back. While Elsa fought waves of terror pulsating throughout her body, Wynn behaved as though they were going on a holiday. "Talk about childish behavior," Elsa snapped.

"We'll get them, Mountain Kate. Don't you worry."

For the first time, it sank in. Mountain Kate, Hurricane Nell and all the rest of them were fakes. *She* was the real one. She, with no horse, no gun, no posse, no Papa, no brains at all. None.

At the shop, Wynn asked, "May I have this?" A thick oak barrel stave leaned against a stall.

Gruffly, the blacksmith said, "Take it."

"And this?" Wynn picked up a sturdy shovel handle, minus the shovel.

"Go ahead. Anything else?" The man's wiry eyebrows drew together, extending the length of his forehead, half hiding his black, glaring eyes. Elsa clearly read his message: there'd better not be.

Wynn was hefting a pitchfork. She caught the man's menacing look and rested the fork against the wall. "No, thank you. Can't really use it."

They tossed the stave and handle behind the back of the single-seated buggy, then stopped by the jail to check for any recent news on the bank theft. Outside the door, the short, rail-thin deputy leaned comfortably in a chair tilted back against the wall, his hat shading his eyes, his arms locked together across his chest. Two other men, hats low, lounged with him, adding to the tobacco stains encircling their feet. Elsa swallowed hard and kept her eyes glued on their faces.

"Deputy," Wynn asked, halting the buggy. "Have they caught the bank robbers yet?"

Elsa closed her eyes. She was a fool for having quit her job and for allowing Wynn to convince her that this was a good thing to do.

"No, ma'am. Posse came in about midnight last night. Didn't see any signs up in the Black Hills. Sheriff thinks they took off for the Badlands. Posse's headed there now."

He nodded politely to the ladies as they thanked him and pulled away.

Leaving the horse and buggy out front, they returned to the boardinghouse to pack. In their room, Elsa said, "We should have gone with the posse."

"Fat chance. We're women."

"So's Mountain Kate. But she carried more than a paltry barrel stave and a shovel handle."

"A good whack upside the head will slow anybody down," Wynn said confidently.

Elsa shivered. "If you can get close enough."

"The gang's smaller by two."

"That's a relief to know."

Elsa took a seat by the window, pensively watching people driving by. She said, "I don't know a darned thing about living outdoors, let alone camping out at night. For all I know I could get jumped by a mountain lion." She rose, closing the short distance to where Wynn stood fussing with her hair before the dresser mirror. "They weigh more than I do, they run faster and their nails are a hell of a lot longer than mine. I don't think a cuff alongside any lion's head is going to do me any good." As she stepped closer yet to Wynn, Wynn raised her hands in mock protection before her chest. Elsa's gaze bore into her. "And what makes you think those outlaws did head for the Badlands. Just because Deston told that empty-headed deputy so?"

"You and I are going to look for them in the Black Hills, right over there." Wynn gestured in a westerly direction with her chin.

Angrily, Elsa stamped her foot. "Good God, Wynn. I know which way west is. You're crazy if you think those thieves are going to hang around here just waiting for two women to show up and capture them? 'Oh, please, sir, would you be good enough to come with us? We need the money, and you're worth a lot. Just get into your saddle so that Wynn doesn't hit you with that dangerous stave she's holding in her hand. There, that's a good outlaw. Oh, yes, and could I have your gun, please? What a kind man.' What *crap,* Wynn."

Wynn wrapped her arms around Elsa. "Oh, now, sweetie."

Elsa pulled away. "Don't 'sweetie' me. We're not that special of friends."

"I am."

"Like hell." Oh, how she loved that word! "A rubdown doesn't give anybody the right to put somebody else's life in danger."

"Yeah, could be a problem."

"What, the rubdowns we give each other? You gonna tell me now that mine are no good anymore?"

Wynn drew Elsa to the bed. "No, I'm not going to tell you that. I was referring to the danger. I know it's there. I know how bad it can be. Here, forget that for a minute. Lie down beside me."

"I don't need a backrub right now. I need to think about staying alive. I've lost my mind."

"You haven't lost your mind, and neither have I. Please, Elsa, lie down with me. I won't give you a backrub if you don't want one."

"I don't!"

"All right, then. It won't happen. There is something else though."

"What?" Elsa lay unyielding as a telegraph pole.

"Relax."

"I am relaxed. You're going to talk me into something. I can feel it. Well, the answer is no!"

Wynn gave her an enormous smile. "You know me well."

"Too well, I'm beginning to think. You're too dangerous to be with, to spend time with. I'd be better off going back home. Now!"

She began to sit up, but Wynn held her down. "I won't talk about going after those men."

"Good."

"For at least thirty minutes."

"*Wynn!*"

"Maybe even longer."

"It'd better be. I can't stand listening to it anymore. I don't feel good, Wynn. My stomach . . ."

Wynn took a deep breath, exhaling slowly. "I know you have a sensitive stomach. Haven't I been patient with that?"

Wynn had. Elsa used to complain about her stomach all the time and not once did Wynn ever say, "Oh, shut up, I've heard enough."

Wynn said instead, "I've been thinking."

"Don't I know that?" Elsa released several clenched muscles in her arms and legs. She stopped grinding her teeth.

"It's about us."

A shot of fear pumped into her chest. Wynn wouldn't dream of going after those outlaws alone, would she? No, that wasn't what she was going to say. She wasn't going to talk about them for thirty minutes. She started to look at her watch.

"Stop checking the time. I need to have your attention. You know, like if you were in the audience and I was riding by."

Elsa's anger collapsed as Wynn gave her a lopsided grin Elsa had never seen before. It threw her heart into a new rhythm. "You were beautiful. You still are. I like you, you devil."

"Elsa, what do you think of — ?" Wynn broke off. A sudden coughing spell forced her to sit up and swing her legs off the bed so that she could breathe better.

"Are you all right?" Elsa slapped her smartly on the back.

Wynn nodded, her violent hacking receding. "Just a little tickle. Comes on me sometimes when I get a little nervous."

When had Wynn ever been nervous? Then she should be coughing to death over her outlaw plan, Elsa thought.

They settled down again, lying side by side, Wynn leaning over Elsa the way she always did before beginning a backrub, and sometimes — often, actually — front rub. "You were asking?"

"I wonder if you thought —" The coughing kicked

in as violently as had the first furious bout. She hacked and fought for breath but remained where she was.

"You'd better sit up," Elsa said. She was scared. Wynn looked awfully red in the face.

Wynn stammered, "If you . . ." Cough, cough. Her breath had nearly left her.

"Wynn, stop it. It's not worth it."

". . . would like to kiss me now." The coughing ceased.

Paralyzed by the suggestion, Elsa envisioned her lips pressing against Wynn's. The terror of going after bandits still whirled in her brain. The thoughts became interlaced. She felt claustrophobic. "It's too . . . much, Wynn. There's just too much for me to think about."

"I feel like it's time we just thought of each other for a while," Wynn whispered. "We need to rejoin ourselves." Her steady breathing caressed Elsa's cheek.

The fear of pursuing bandits receded. In its place came the crashing of Elsa's heart while her head rapidly filled with cobwebs. The kiss. Think only of the kiss, she thought. "Is that right?" she managed to squeak. "Do you . . . want to talk about it, again? I'm sure it's confusing for you." And me, she thought, and me, but I'm still for it. Lingering thoughts of deadly men dissipated.

"I don't want to talk at all."

Wynn gazed into Elsa's eyes for several seconds. If either of them was going to draw a line, it would happen at that moment. There were no questionable boundaries in Elsa's mind, and obviously none in

Wynn's as she inched her mouth lower and closer to Elsa's until they touched — slowly, as if one of them might break the spell.

It was a nice kiss: soft and gentle, but nothing close to what Elsa imagined a kiss to be. Not according to the ten-cent novels she'd read. Disappointed, she broke contact. "Not much to it, is there?"

Wynn was puffing like a locomotive. "Why don't you put your arms all the way around me, and I'll move a little closer to you? We'll try it one more time, and this time you move your lips when I move mine."

"What's the point?"

"It feels nice when I do it. You try it." Wynn again softly placed her lips upon Elsa's. Once more she began to move them. Her head was moving some, too. From the side of her mouth, she muttered, "Close your eyes."

Elsa closed her eyes. She moved her lips a little and then a little more, like Wynn was doing. It was more enjoyable moving her lips when Wynn did. The tip of Wynn's tongue lightly touched her teeth. A stirring in her belly increased when she separated her teeth a crack allowing Wynn to slip her tongue farther into her mouth.

Unsure of what to do, Elsa sucked on Wynn's tongue — for just a second.

Wynn grabbed Elsa, drawing her tightly against her chest, driving her tongue deeper into Elsa's mouth. Elsa liked it. She liked it a great deal. It made her want to push her hips against Wynn's.

When she did, she drove her own tongue into Wynn's mouth. Her rising excitement became penetrating, volcanic. She rolled Wynn onto her back and lay heavily upon her, working her legs between Wynn's. Rhythmically, she propelled her body against her darling, darling, darling.

Wynn matched Elsa's cadence, their bodies dancing smoothly and steadily, one with the other. Elsa experimented with different little movements — open-mouthed, she encircled Wynn's lips. Creating a rosebud, Wynn could engulf Elsa's. Elsa breathed heavily, the inhibitions within her gone. She licked Wynn's mouth, teeth, cheeks, ears.

They rolled over again so that Wynn now lay on Elsa, their rhythm increasing. Elsa waited, poised for wherever Wynn's kissing would further transport them.

Wynn's hair hung in ticklish masses against Elsa's face. Elsa reveled in the maddening caresses. Soft, warm feathers seemingly stroked her cheeks and throat.

Wynn broke from Elsa, seeking her nipples easily visible through her blouse, swollen with fervent longing to be touched. Through the cloth, Wynn's lips pressed upon the firm flesh. A flood of liquid heat surged through Elsa's body, its foremost intensity centered squarely between her legs.

She arched her back, driving herself hard against Wynn, lifting them both off the bed with ardent thrusts. Wynn stayed with her, not missing a palpitation, zealously riding the gale.

They floated together, their lips compressed as

one, smearing each other's faces, tips of tongues flicking in and out of mouths and ears.

Tiny bites on Elsa's neck threw her body into savage gyrations, heightening the pulsations still gripping her body. "I can't stand . . . I can't . . ." Wynn gasped, tugging at Elsa as though to fuse Elsa's body with her own.

Their rhythm began to decrease as Elsa slowly cooled. Eventually, their movements ceased. Sweat saturated their clothing. An exciting odor lingered about them. Elsa felt they were a single entity. She remembered thinking that her mama and papa had been like that.

Wynn slid to Elsa's side, nestling against her. Elsa's arms encircled her and Wynn burrowed even deeper.

Elsa ran her fingers through Wynn's hair. "I think kissing should be part of our rubdowns, Wynn."

"I love you, Elsa."

Tranquility filled Elsa's breast. She wasn't afraid. Not of anything. Not right now. She sighed peacefully. "I love you too, special friend. My special, special friend."

"I'd keep you forever if I could," Wynn said.

Elsa pulled her tighter. "You can keep me forever if I can keep you."

"You really mean it?"

"Yes."

"Marriage?"

"Just with you."

"Same here." Wynn paused. "It's strange we haven't kissed before this. Absurd almost."

"Very. Any man and woman would have kissed months ago."

"We aren't a man and woman."

"No," Elsa agreed. "We're not. We're special. Special people wait for the proper time. The right time. Not before."

"No, not before."

They napped until sundown.

CHAPTER FIFTEEN

Elsa woke slowly, reliving her moments with Wynn. By the look of the shadows stretching across the room, it was nearly seven p.m. Wynn was so right. Kissing did make their backrubs more — passionate. Again she heard Wynn saying, "I love you," and Elsa saying the same back, their words making so much sense that Elsa wondered why they didn't think to tell each other long ago.

A knock on the door brought her to full wakefulness. Wynn slept on as though she'd taken too much laudanum. "Who is it?"

"Mrs. Kettle."

Elsa leaped from the bed running her fingers through her hair and straightening her clothing as best as possible. "I'm coming, Mrs. Kettle." She hurried to the door and flung it open.

"You got a telegram a minute ago. Somebody from the office just delivered it. I thought you might want it right away." Having done her duty, she turned briskly on her heel and left.

Since coming to Wawtauk, Elsa had received two telegrams from Mama, each saying the same thing: WAGES NOT ENOUGH STOP RETURN STOP. She opened the envelope expecting to read a similar message. The words were not the same. DESPERATE STOP THREATS STOP FIFTEEN DAYS INCREASE PAY STOP HOUSE LIVES GONE STOP. MAMA. Elsa blinked rapidly rereading the message.

Wynn woke and sat up rubbing the sleep from her eyes. She swung her feet off the side of the bed, seeing the telegram in Elsa's hands. "Your mama?"

Elsa nodded, staring at nothing. "The terms have been changed."

"Why?" Lightning bolts of worry flashed in Wynn's eyes.

"Greed, probably," Elsa answered dully. "Mama must be near hysterical with fear." Just like she was. She and Wynn were foolish not to have started hours ago. Now they would be facing darkness by the time they reached the foothills where trees grew so thick they could get turned around and lost in two minutes. There would be big cats, tall bears, poisonous snakes and killers. These were the enemies standing between Mama's and Elsa's right to live peaceful, normal lives.

157

Elsa sunk to the chair, shivering even though the room was warm. "I don't know if I can shoot those men."

Wynn came over and knelt before her. She placed her hands on Elsa's legs. "We wouldn't shoot anybody."

"We wouldn't have to. They'd shoot us before we got within ten miles of them. That would take care of that wouldn't it?"

"If they shot us, it would."

Elsa looked at Wynn as though they had both lost all common sense or value for their lives. God, the very *thought* of taking such a risk. That's all the whole insane venture was, Elsa thought, a gamble that they could survive, a gamble that they'd find the men, a gamble they had even the remotest possibility of bringing them back alive. And what if there were more members who'd joined the original gang? She refused to consider the possibility and went on to despair at recovering any reward money at all.

She reread the telegram four more times. In fifteen days, the blackmailers were increasing the payments. Mama's and her money was no longer enough. For whatever reason, "they" would soon burn the house and take Mama's life, and then "they" would find her and take hers.

She wadded the telegram into a tight little ball. "I hate my papa." Dropping her head, she clutched the telegram tightly with both hands, gasping for breath and fighting the ever-present, vexatious reaction she had toward blatant fear: nausea.

She looked at Wynn. "We'd better get going

before all the light's gone. You pack for us. I'll go see Mrs. Kettle and beg for food. She can't be all that hard-hearted."

Mrs. Kettle gave them enough food for five days. She wasn't kind about it, slamming each piece of cheese, bread and salted meat into a basket before shoving it toward Elsa. "It's only because I thought the world of you, Elsa, that I'm doing this, but I feel like you deserted me. I counted on you."

"I'm sorry, Mrs. Kettle. I truly am."

Ten minutes later the two women stored Mrs. Kettle's vittles and two small suitcases packed with warm clothing beneath the buggy's seat. They wore their heaviest dresses and stockings and pulled their sunbonnets tight to their heads to ward off the evening's damp air. "I told Mrs. Kettle we're going camping. I know she doesn't believe me."

Wynn moved close to Elsa's side. "We'll be fine," she said. "I promise you. I was raised on a ranch, remember?"

Buck, their gelding, looked sound, pulling them along as though they weighed nothing. The buggy seemed less able, with plenty of mileage on it. Elsa hoped it'd last the week. But it might not be for just one week, she thought.

The sinking sun streaked the sky with infinite rays of yellows, reds and oranges as they headed for the Black Hills.

Wynn tried to cheer Elsa. "We'll be back here so soon it'll be like we'd never left." Handling the reins, she clucked her tongue, and Buck increased his speed to an easy canter.

Elsa scowled into the night. Mountain Kate was full of horse hay. She'd be scared, too, if she were here.

They reached the foothills at two a.m., their way lit by a brilliant, full moon. A road once used for logging, now populated only by occasional hunters or picnic parties, wound its way upward for three miles. The route became increasingly jolting and tiresome. It ended abruptly, turning into a little-used trail. Wynn jumped from the buggy and lit the lantern. "I'll check for another way." She walked off, the night thrust back by the lamp's golden glow.

Elsa let out a frightful scream, spinning Wynn around. The buggy tipped slowly to its right until the rear wagon wheel cracked in two and the carriage rested at a peculiar angle to the ground. Buck fought against the unfamiliar pull of the tack. Elsa lay upside down near the front seat.

Wynn set down the lantern and ran back to grab Buck's halter before he started dragging the disabled buggy. "Easy, boy," she said. "Easy."

Slightly dazed, Elsa slowly got to her feet and moved away from the danger. "Is the horse going to bolt?"

Wynn unhitched him in lightning time. She stroked his cheeks and neck and shoulders, speaking softly to him. "Not now. Are you all right?" She turned to Elsa, brushing her off, checking her over.

"I'm fine," Elsa said, examining herself as well. "Look, my dress has a terrible tear in it." At the waist the skirt had ripped half free of the blouse.

"You can pin it." Wynn gently pulled and tugged at Elsa's skirt.

"Did you bring any pins?"

Wynn hesitated. "Actually, no."

"A needle."

"No."

"Thread? Anything?"

"Didn't think to."

"Well, let's see if we can't at least fix the buggy." Elsa fetched the lantern and held it up. "Wheel's finished. Axle's snapped right in two. We can't fix that." She saw again Mama's frantic telegram, and a tidal surge of terror invaded her being. "Can we ride double?"

"If Buck'll let us."

"Then we'll bring the grain, the food and the weapons and leave the rest."

Wynn grabbed two sweaters from the suitcases and they pulled them on. The air was considerably cooler at this hour and height. The woods had closed in on them a mile back.

Another scream filled the woods. "What was that?" Elsa whipped her head back and forth. She strained her eyes in a vain attempt to penetrate the shadowy darkness, the moon only barely casting enough light through the forest to see by.

"Cat," Wynn answered.

"I'm scared," Elsa said flatly.

"I'm ready to run, myself," Wynn admitted.

The confession rattled Elsa to her bones. "Really?"

"Not real bad."

"Gee, Wynn, that makes me feel a whole lot better."

They helped each other onto Buck's back and rode on. Wynn sat in front, Elsa behind, their supplies tucked between them. Elsa also carried the lantern, holding it first with one arm straight out so that it didn't touch the horse and then switching arms. In this manner they slowly made their way forward, climbing ever higher into the mountains.

An unbearable ache set into Elsa's arms and shoulders from straight-arming the lantern for so long. "We're going to have to stop soon," she said.

Readily, Wynn agreed. "This looks as good a place as any."

They rested against a tree, the lantern close beside them, its beam holding back the night. Elsa clutched the barrel stave in one hand while holding Buck's reins with the other. "I'm stiff," she said.

"I am too." Wynn rested the shovel handle across her lap. "I can't believe it after all the riding I've done in my life." She sounded discouraged.

Elsa set down the stave and held Wynn's hand.

Neither slept. There were too many rustling sounds in the surrounding brush and in the trees above.

"I never knew so much life carried on at night," Elsa said.

"You don't necessarily want to know what it is, either," Wynn answered.

Elsa took up the stave again.

Before morning broke, they were astride Buck's back. His body gave welcomed warmth to Elsa's inner thighs. She wished she were wearing men's pants. She knew she'd be more comfortable no matter how ridiculous she looked. This morning she'd spent several more minutes squatting in the woods than she normally would. She was able to eat a small piece of cheese, but that was all.

For hours they traveled the only detectable trail. "Look." Wynn pulled Buck to a halt and pointed to a tiny object in the pathway. "Matchstick laying there, isn't it?"

"Think they came this way?"

"Somebody did. Can't be posse tracks though. The trail's not worn down enough for a whole bunch of riders. Three men might leave this small trail. Another ten would tear up the earth."

"Those outlaws know exactly where they're going. How'd the law miss them?"

"Don't know. Don't care. Maybe somebody drew them off. Maybe they're camping far from here. I just hope we don't miss the bastards."

Virgin timber had once covered this area. The tall trees had been logged out by the timber barons. Great gullies of wide stumps and ugly scarred earth eroding away year by year made their trek almost impossible at times. Miles of waste, discarded branches and limbs still lay in high tangled heaps, impeding their progress and robbing them of precious energy.

Frequently, the terrain abruptly changed, forcing them to walk, leading Buck down steep ravines and across rapid streams before ascending others. They were high now and dropping hundreds of feet only to reclimb hundreds more before reaching the next mountain. After dipping in and out of dozens of such ravines, five nights later they slid off the horse's back and sat unmoving where they landed.

Elsa gasped, "We have wandered all over these mountains. This trail, that trail. Nothing! We'll never find them. Probably the posse's already nailed them. Mama..." Her voice broke off as she doggedly refused to shed a single tear.

"Quit complaining," Wynn snapped. "I'm from

California, remember? Dad used to talk about outlaws. They were never where they were supposed to be when you went after them, and I'm betting Dad's right again. Why in hell ride clear to the Badlands when there's a million places to bury yourself right here. The place is loaded with ravines and there's plenty of water. Dad's right, and so are we." She rose to step behind a bush to relieve herself and tripped over a branch, falling to her knees.

Elsa got up and hauled her to her feet. "We could just give up and go back to Staten Island. Those crooks might not really mean it." She didn't believe her own words, but she was so exhausted and terribly hungry.

"We're gonna get there," Wynn vowed. She wore a wicked sneer, twisting her lips unnaturally and baring her teeth as though she could clamp down upon the throats of the bandits and rip them open. "I'm gonna get there. After all this trouble, I deserve to get there." She looked hard at Elsa. "And if you don't start showing a little hope, I'm gonna have to work twice as hard as I am. You keep your mama's face before you at all times. And think about how your papa crumbled at your feet."

Elsa shuddered, fighting terror and tears. "You're right," she answered softly, lamely. "I'm a coward. I do my best to cover it, but I'm still a coward. I'm not even thinking of Mama now."

"Shut your damn mouth, Elsa. Go take a walk or something. I'm tired of your attitude. It's making it hard as hell to think."

Wynn limped painfully away rubbing her impaired arm and fingers.

Elsa's embarrassment was unbearable. "I'm sorry,

Wynn. Forget what I said." She put her arms around Wynn, speaking with a confidence she didn't come close to feeling. "We'll get there, my dear, dear darling. We will get there and we'll take their guns and take back the money, and Mama and you and me will be just fine. We'll follow them to Oregon if we have to." She sounded like fictitious Mountain Kate, but the words seemed to put some light back into Wynn's eyes.

"I get tired, you know."

"I know you do, Wynn. Here, lean on me for a while. I can help you." Elsa wished they still carried the lantern, but the fuel had run out days ago. They slept one at a time throughout the night.

They had stopped late each night since beginning their journey, alternating handling the reins and the weapons and supplies, riding when they could, dozing restlessly, sometimes both falling asleep at the same time. When this happened, they quarreled. They were scared. They could have been attacked through their own recklessness.

They had stingily but intelligently rationed their foodstuffs since the start of their trip, not knowing exactly how long they'd be gone. If they didn't stumble onto the outlaws within the next couple of dadys, they'd be forced to turn back. Five days' rations didn't begin to cover what they needed for such an arduous undertaking. Buck, too, was showing irritation at eating so little grain or grass.

They stopped at the streams, refreshing themselves with deliciously cold, clear water while keeping their bellies falsely full.

The next afternoon, after having climbed over and under debris, clambered off and on Buck and fallen three more times, Wynn's fortitude finally cracked. On their next break, she said, "I wouldn't mind turning back. Not anymore."

Elsa heard her clearly, deciding that neither would she. Wynn looked like she hadn't seen civilization in fifteen years with her hair in tangles and her face covered with grime. Their clothing had been reduced to tattered rags from clasping bushes and unexpected branches. Elsa gave Wynn one of her backrub kinds of kisses that Wynn didn't resist at all. After that, their spirits perked up for a few hours, and they continued onward.

By God's grace or uncanny luck, just off the trail that evening they passed an important indicator that they were, again, on someone's track. "See? One of them took a crap right there." Elsa pointed.

"Christ, the least he could do is throw a rock over it. Come on."

Traveling along the ridge of one of the smaller mountains hidden in an amphitheater of much larger ones, just to hear herself talk, Elsa asked, "How long have we been on this trail?"

"Four hundred years."

"Ha ha."

"Nine days."

"Seems longer."

Wynn nodded. Elsa assumed Wynn was answering affirmatively, but what Wynn had done was doze off, held on Buck's back by Elsa's strong arms around her. She took the reins from Wynn's hands.

Seeing and hearing nothing unusual — the animals' sounds had become ordinary noises to her ears — she made the big decision for them both. They were going to have to take a chance and sleep tonight whether they wanted to or not. They were practically already asleep with their eyes open. If there was going to be trouble, sleeping or awake, they wouldn't be alert enough to do anything about it. Not in the shape they were in. Having traveled so far for so many days with little food, and almost nonstop, they had to be nearing something, someone, someplace. Nothing went on forever. Her eyes crossed involuntarily as she fought to keep them focused. Slumber pressed down upon her. Lying beneath one of these mountains would be easier to endure.

Elsa thanked God that Wynn had been raised out West and that she knew a few things about tracking from having gone out on the trail with her dad a few times. She was able to read the more notable signs and by doing so had carefully guided them in a criss-cross fashion over large tracts of land by observing the direction streams flowed, by the moss growing on tree trunks or where particular plants chose to sprout. Mountain Kate, Hurricane Nell, Wild Bill Hickok and the whole bunch of them were beginning to look like dolts next to Wynn's legitimate knowledge of the outdoors.

Some distance away, a man's voice broke out in raucous laugher. The sound came from over there. No, over that way.

Elsa pulled Buck up short, tightening her grip around Wynn. She sat immobile and was instantly and completely alert.

CHAPTER SIXTEEN

"Wynn," she whispered. She gave Wynn a slight squeeze.

Wynn raised her chin from her chest. "Huh?"

"Don't say a word. Just listen."

They sat stone still. A half-mile a way or so, they both heard them: two men laughing and talking. Elsa stared hard in the sound's direction. Wynn was just as vigilant, just as tense. "Posse?"

"Maybe." Buck snorted, and they dismounted immediately. Limping badly, Wynn hurried to cover Buck's nose. She rubbed his nostrils and scratched his ears. "Shhh, Buck, shhh. Good boy." Buck quieted while they continued listening. Elsa didn't move a muscle. Wynn only stroked the horse.

The men's voices faded off to their left. Buck's ears perked up as he swung his head in that direction. Wynn grabbed his nostrils and pinched his nose. If those men were on horses, old Buck didn't need to be greeting his brethren.

They remained nearly motionless for another half-hour, listening for additional voices, Elsa rubbing Buck's sides, Wynn caressing his head and nose, whispering so low that only Buck could hear her.

"What do you think?" Wynn finally murmured.

"I'd like to move away from this horse dung, that's what I think." Elsa spoke less quietly than Wynn. Buck had let loose some time ago, and Elsa could still feel where it had splattered her legs.

"Shhh. They'll hear you."

"Yeah? Who cares?"

"I do."

"Sorry." Elsa realized her common sense was deserting her. Being careless could kill them both.

Wynn didn't look like she believed her, but she accepted her apology. "We need to think of something."

"No kidding."

Wynn put a balled fist on her hip. "You know, Elsa, sometimes I don't think I like you."

"When's that?"

Wynn paused. "When I recall, I'll tell you. Your eyes have a way of taking the fight out of me. It isn't fair."

Elsa smiled. "Let's lay out a plan." The last hour's tension was lessening. It was good to feel only exhausted and frightened again, not exhausted, frightened and angry all at the same time.

They tied Buck to a bush where he began munching on its leaves and nosing the ground, searching for grass. The women rested on a nearby rock. "Our best weapon will be surprise."

Elsa concurred. "I wonder why they're still so close to town."

"Elsa, we've been riding almost nonstop for eight days and nights. They aren't that close. They must have a shack up here."

"What if they have a dog? We won't be able to get near them if they have a dog."

"Outlaws don't have dogs, do they?"

"I haven't any idea what outlaws have other than guns and bullets."

"Let's assume they haven't got dogs. Dogs would only be trouble."

Wynn repositioned herself on the rock so that she could pull her knees to her chest. She wrapped her arms around them. "A plan," she said.

"We should have been thinking of one all along."

"Could you?"

"I can't think at all. Not even about food, and that's on my mind a lot." They fell silent, and Elsa finally said, "I need to throw up."

Wynn looked downright disgusted. "For crying out loud, Elsa, get a hold of yourself. We're about to try something that could get us both killed. I can't go in there alone and get them. We both need to be there and mindful."

That did it. Elsa hustled off the rock and behind some bushes just off the trail. She cleaned up with leaves she pulled from bushes.

Returning, she said, "I'm kind of dizzy."

"Can't argue that."

Elsa swallowed Wynn's unwillingness to sympathize. She always had before. They'd talked about it just a few days ago. Mama would have sent her straight to bed and brought her a cup of tea. Wynn wasn't Mama. Elsa wasn't a little girl. She was a frightened woman accompanied by another frightened woman who counted on her help and strength. Sometimes Elsa felt confident. Most times, she wanted only to run home to Mama's arms.

She leaned heavily against the rock. "Give me a minute."

Wynn examined the surrounding forest and dense foliage while Elsa collected herself.

"I wish I was brave. Why aren't I brave, Wynn?"

"Oh, shut up." Wynn limped away from her, rubbing her arm. Elsa's face burned with shame as she stared after her. Wynn trembled, and her hands shook like leaves in the wind.

"You're right," Elsa said. "Stupid question. You're probably not half as brave as you put on. Probably not even half as brave as me."

Wynn's face darkened. "I'm getting close to telling you the times when I don't like you."

"Never mind. We need to come up with a plan."

"That's all we need to talk about."

"That's right. We'll probably only get one chance." That said, Elsa's stomach again knotted tighter than a hangman's noose, and she doubled over.

"Again?" Wynn remarked impatiently.

"Nope," Elsa lied through clenched teeth. "I just spotted a pretty stone." She retrieved the first pebble she could lay her fingers on and handed it to Wynn. "See?" She was able to sit upright.

Wynn ignored the stone. "Throw that away. We need to think sharp now."

"Surprise attack is the only thing we have."

"One-shot deal."

"Let's hope no shots at all." Elsa's voice shook.

Wynn slipped her arm around Elsa's waist. "There won't be, sweetie. We'll be real careful, and then we'll go home."

Elsa leaned against her. Closing her eyes, she saw herself face down, draped over a saddle, and wished that they were a thousand miles away.

That night the moonglow was masked by dark clouds. Beneath the canopy of trees, the forest was black as an abandoned coal mine and equally as forbidding. The winds blew strongly, whistling through the branches above and rustling the low-lying, thick underbrush.

Elsa couldn't see her hand in front of her face, nor could she see Wynn, standing only a yard away. She checked Buck once more assuring herself that he was securely tied. Taking a deep breath, she said, "Okay. Let's go."

Before the day's light had faded completely, each of them had memorized the terrain, their eyes penetrating the woods as deeply possible. They tied their hats on tight, pulled on their sweaters and clutched their weapons in their hands. It was time to move closer to the spot where they believed they had heard the men. Once there, they wouldn't move until they detected more voices. They relied upon the wind and the leaves' rustling to cover their movements.

Within five yards, Elsa's skirt snagged on something. "Wait a minute," she muttered, reaching to free her skirt. "Let's go."

"Wait, my hat brim's caught." There was a pause, then, "Okay." A few seconds later, Wynn again murmured, "Hold on. I'm snagged again."

Another minute passed, then both stopped to free their skirts from grasping bushes and branches.

"We have to get rid of these clothes," Wynn said. "Damn, now I've torn my sleeve. We must be hung up in some kind of a thorn patch."

"You mean, get undressed?"

"Just your hat, sweater and dress."

"We'll freeze to death."

"It's summertime, Elsa."

Elsa stripped to her personals, feeling more exposed than she had ever felt in her life. She wrapped her clothing into a tight ball and jammed it inside the rear of her drawers feeling almost as though she were preparing to ride another bronco.

"Tuck your dress . . ."

"Got it," Elsa said. She was shivering badly, more from fear than the cool night air.

Unencumbered by excess clothing, they were better able to negotiate the thickets. Within the first two minutes they'd been on the trail, Wynn released an unseen, unexpected, tiny branch that lashed Elsa across the cheek, stinging her as though she'd been horse-whipped. She muffled a cry with her hand. After that, she held up her hand, fingers spread in front of her face at all times. "Are you there?" she murmured every few feet.

"Right here," Wynn replied softly.

Inch by inch, they made their way toward their target. "What if they come back to the same spot?" Elsa asked.

"We'll freeze like deer," Wynn answered. "They won't see us if they don't expect us and we don't do anything to draw attention to ourselves."

Elsa wouldn't. She'd set up like concrete till she turned ninety if she had to.

A far-off guffaw drew their attention eastward. "Over this way," Wynn said.

"Don't lose me." Elsa trembled at the sound of the man's voice. Wynn's cold hand unexpectedly touched her, and she nearly shrieked.

"Grab my hand," Wynn whispered. "Don't let go. Stick close."

Elsa did.

"No talking."

No problem there, either. Elsa's throat had nearly closed in her rising panic. She took long, steady, deep breaths to settle herself as she stumbled through the darkness. Unseen boughs raked her exposed skin.

Wynn continued in the lead, Elsa floundering along behind her. An occasional sudden jerk on Elsa's hand suggested Wynn was fighting for balance too.

Laughter echoed throughout the woods, followed by loud, angry voices. A horse nickered. Elsa's eyes were opened wide as though this would allow her to hear better, even though she still could see nothing.

She bumped into Wynn who had paused to listen. Wynn slid her hand up Elsa's arm and around her neck. Elsa shivered from her frigid touch. Summer or not, it was cold in these mountains.

Wynn's mouth drew close to Elsa's ear. "I don't

think they're a half-mile away. How about we crawl the rest of the way?"

Elsa agreed. Crawling would be far better, for her waning courage was barely holding her upright.

It was much slower going on their knees, Elsa's becoming sore knobs in no time from roots and stones that pressed like vicious little enemies into her kneecaps. Thank God, at least at night it was too cold for bugs at this altitude.

Several times they were forced to retreat and try a different way, unable to penetrate the thick bushes. The wind whipped the foliage more strongly, a welcomed blessing to Elsa. She wondered what Wynn was thinking, up there in the front, leading them, being first. She prayed they weren't making any more noise than an animal might.

Wynn stopped and again, unable to see her, Elsa ran into her. She exhaled slowly until her heart steadied.

Through the darkness ahead, she spotted the glow of a fire. They had reached the camp, and that was no posse sitting around that fire.

They eased back a few yards and rested. Their plan was so utterly bizarre, so utterly ridiculous, it just might work. It *had* to work.

"We need to put on our dresses," Elsa whispered against Wynn's ear.

Wynn shook her head vigorously.

Elsa pulled Wynn's ear hard to her mouth. "They'll ravage us."

Again, Wynn indicated no. "They'll be too surprised to do anything. Probably think we're ghosts."

"I won't do it."

"Then wait here." By dim shadows Elsa watched Wynn move off.

Gritting her teeth, Elsa followed. Without looking, Wynn reached around and patted Elsa, catching her in the eye. Elsa grimaced, fighting her tearing eye, and slapped away Wynn's hand. Wynn started forward again.

They paused twenty yards from the fire and watched four men seated around the small blaze, reclining against their saddles. Four men! Elsa had been thinking only in terms of three.

The outlaws talked, their voices rising and falling. Although there were four horses tethered to a line hitch, they waited to see if any more people were nearby or if these men would get up and start wandering around. They'd guessed right about the dogs. If there had been any around, she and Wynn would've been dead long before.

Twenty minutes passed before Elsa felt Wynn shift. The outlaws stayed put, appearing relaxed and unconcerned about their hideout. No one came out of the shack. They had to know the posse was far off their trail.

Wynn fumbled around until she felt the shovel handle in Elsa's hand. Wynn directed Elsa's hand to the barrel stave she held, letting Elsa know that she too was ready. It was time to put their scheme, idiotic beyond reason or intelligence, into motion.

Elsa heard Wynn breathe deeply. She did so herself, filling her lungs until her chest hurt. No dress, no real weapons, nothing but lunacy to carry them through.

They sneaked forward fifteen yards. Elsa could

now clearly see Wynn's outline. She stood stealthily, holding the stave casually in her right hand. She looked as sinister as a child's babydoll and downright laughable with her oversized backside where her clothing filled her underdrawers. Elsa took a similar pose, her knees barely able to support her. As cold as she was, sweat rolled off her face and body.

The group's mounts lifted their heads and looked their way. They pricked their ears. Two of them nickered. The horses were giving away their position.

Keeping with the plan, with the added problem of one more criminal, they stepped boldly forward, no longer mindful of the noise they created.

The bandits were instantly on their feet, and as Elsa and Wynn emerged from the woods into the light of the fire, four pistols were pointed straight at them. Elsa stared down the barrel of one. The hole at the end looked as big as a cannon's.

CHAPTER SEVENTEEN

Using the stave to support herself, Wynn leaned casually against it much as she might use a cane. "Evening, boys. Got any coffee?"

If the money was here, Elsa thought the outlaws a mighty sorry looking lot for having eighty thousand dollars in their possession. With the exception of one young man, the rest needed shaves and their beards trimmed. Every gang member's hat was a battered old wreck, and their clothing was caked with dirt. They all smelled as though they hadn't touched a bar of soap since birth.

Having studied the bounty hunter's poster a hundred times since retrieving it from the street weeks ago, Elsa knew who each one was. The oldest with the long dirty, white beard was Toss Baker. He'd ridden down Wynn and cut her when his spur struck her face. Next to him was Jake Colben, the one who'd rolled Elsa to the ground. He looked about fifteen years old. Another man resembling Jake, but older and taller, was Brad Colben, likely Jake's brother. Who the fourth man at the fire was she didn't know. He hadn't been in the poster.

Other than astonishment registering on their faces, not a man moved. Not a man spoke. The pistol's barrel opening grew large. Elsa imagined herself tumbling into it.

Wynn sauntered to the fire, peering into a pot hanging over the flames. "Smells good," she said. She winked at Jake and touched the hat of the stranger.

"What the hell?" Toss Baker reacted first, his heavy moustache concealing his mouth as he cursed. The bandits were coming out of their shock.

It was past time for Elsa to move. Fueled with stark fear and desperation, she and Wynn simultaneously let out a vicious caterwaul, each clubbing the man nearest her. Toss Baker and Jake Colben dropped their guns as they went down, knocked cold by two pitiful weapons wielded by two determined women filled with the brawn of a man driving a railroad spike.

Before the unfortunate ones hit the ground, Elsa swung at Brad Colben and Wynn hit the stranger. They too, took stunning blows. Brad fell to one knee still holding his pistol. "Get 'em, Sugarfoot," he gasped.

Elsa brought the stave down against Brad's wrist sending his gun off to the left. Sugarfoot had fared much better, the whack by the shovel handle only clobbering his shoulder. He aimed his gun at Wynn. In his nervous excitement he missed her by an inch before lunging toward her.

Without considering the danger, Elsa moved in close to stop him. She caught him at the base of his skull, and he folded like an accordion.

Wynn hurried around collecting the guns, emptying the chambers of two before flinging the weapons far into the woods. She passed Elsa a pistol, who wanted no part of it, and then tied the extra bullets in a pouch at the waist of her slip before recovering her pistol and training it on the dazed outlaws. By now they were all sitting up, stupefied and bruised. Wynn clutched the gun with both hands, her grip perfectly steady, her injured arm having no effect upon her handling the pistol. The weapon roared and a bullet kicked up dust not two inches from Toss Baker's boot.

"Anybody moves a muscle, and I'll shoot you right between your eyes." She stood straddle-legged, her torso strong and unyielding. Only the slightest suggestion of sanity lingered in her eyes where the firelight flickered and her unclad skin glowed red from the flames.

Elsa marveled at Wynn's nerve and the growing strength of her body. She was being restored before Elsa's eyes. She duplicated Wynn's assured stance, pointing her gun at the men, saying, "Good idea," believing it not a good idea at all but one she could live with if she had to.

Toss Baker screamed like a crazy man. "Goddamn

it, Sugarfoot, you were supposed to draw off the posse."

The one called Sugarfoot yelled back. "I did. Look at them, you asshole. They ain't no posse. They're two *girls*." He laughed at the men's plight, phlegm rattling in his throat, his voice deep and burred. "Lucky shot, lady. Now gimme that thing before you shoot yourself right in your pretty little foot."

As he rose to reach for Wynn, Elsa moved near him and brought her weapon down hard, cracking the barrel across his fingers. Drenched in fear, the hated feeling provided her with excess strength, and the clout was a punishing one.

Sugarfoot snatched his hand away, cradling it with the other. "Ouch. Goddamn it, girl. Are you crazy?"

Elsa quickly backed away. She had recklessly stepped too close to him to begin with, but by God, when people started messing with her lady . . .

"Elsa, look in the shack. See if the money's in there." Wynn cocked her gun again. The men's eyes widened as her finger tightened against the trigger.

"You take the money, lady, and you're dead," Baker said.

Elsa swung her pistol toward him. "Shut up!"

He did, giving Elsa a sense of power she had never before experienced. Suddenly she felt like she could handle them all. "You even think about . . ." She heard her voice trembling and stopped mid-sentence. She'd wait a little while before saying too much. She'd be more settled by then. Maybe.

A lantern sat just outside the door. She lighted it with matches from a box beside it and cautiously entered the building with her gun cocked and ready.

181

She lifted the lantern illuminating the shack's interior. The place was a sty. There was no table. Dirty dishes, cups and utensils were randomly stacked in the center of the floor. The men apparently slept on the floor as well as ate there. The walls were bare. Cracks could be seen between every board. She shifted the light and saw two canvas bags in one corner. She ripped them open. The money! "Got it," she yelled and scuttled from the cabin.

"Anything from the train? Jewelry?" Wynn asked.

"Nothing else," Elsa said, returning to Wynn's side.

Blood ran down the faces of Toss Baker and Jake Colben from the blows they had suffered, making them look hideous in the firelight. Their ten-gallons had only barely saved their brains from being caved in altogether. She could hardly believe she had been responsible for the way they looked. She killed the lantern's flame and dropped the sacks at Wynn's feet.

Wynn took charge, instantly relieving Elsa, whose moment of power was rapidly slipping away. Wynn spoke harshly to the older Colben, "Get some rope. Tie the rest up. Hands behind their backs, feet bound together, then hands and feet tied together."

Colben glowered at her. "Don't give a man much of a chance, do you, lady?"

"Get some rope, or I'll flay you and use your own skin." Her gun roared again, this time shooting into the flames. Sparks flew everywhere as the bullet harmlessly ricocheted off into the woods. But every man threw himself flat to the ground.

Baker and Sugarfoot began crawling on hands and knees as fast as they could toward the edge of the forest. "Stop," Wynn shouted. Another shot thudded into a tree next to Baker's head. The bandits halted and moved back into the circle of light. "Get the damn rope."

Sugarfoot pulled his saddle closer to him, releasing a lariat from a rear saddle string.

Elsa watched each man before her. She looked at scum. Yes, it just might be possible for her to shoot a man. These types were the kind that had made her life one big pile of horse manure back home and now here. She drew a bead on Sugarfoot who was tying the others. She said, "You tie those thieving alley cats up real good, mister, or you're gonna make me mad." The more she talked the more livid she became. A rage slowly built within her, similar to that which she had felt when Mama burned her mail. "Tie it *real* good!" she said as her fury mounted.

"Get back, Sugarfoot," Wynn ordered when the three were tied. She checked the ropes. "Redo his," she said, indicating Jake's bindings.

"I told you to do it right," Elsa screamed at him. "I'll shoot you." She pointed the gun at Sugarfoot's chest.

Fear bathed his face. He held up a hand as though it could stop a bullet. "I'll fix it. It was a mistake. I'll fix it." Elsa's gun was still pointed at him. She lifted her thumb to draw back the hammer.

Wynn stepped beside her. "Elsa, I think we should wait on shooting them."

"*Why?*"

"So that they can see what it's like to be afraid for a change. So that we can steal from them."

Elsa resurfaced from some deep, murky place in

183

her mind. She was losing her lucidity. She eased her thumb off the hammer but didn't lower the gun an inch.

"Now drag these boys away from each other," Wynn commanded Sugarfoot. "They're too close."

"Don't see how two itty-bitty girls can swing a club the way you two do and take out four men. It ain't right. Women oughtn't be behavin' in such heathen ways," Sugarfoot grumbled loudly as he retied Jake's ropes.

Again Wynn checked the knots. She passed her gun to Elsa and bound him too.

"Now what?" Baker raged. His face contorted into deep gullies and gashes around his eyes, his unkempt beard jutting out as he demanded answers.

"We leave at dawn," Wynn said. Moving back several yards, she retrieved her dress and slipped it over her head, discarding her hat.

"Get dressed, Elsa," she said, taking charge of both guns.

Taking turns, they finished the pot's contents and washed it down with water from the men's canteens. Elsa had never eaten anything that looked so disgusting and tasted so delicious in her life.

They stood guard until dawn broke, remaining on their feet throughout the night and leaning against a tree, an assurance they'd stay awake this way.

Trussed up like turkeys, the outlaws themselves only dozed intermittently. Upon awaking, they whined without letup about their bindings, cramps in their shoulders and their hands going to sleep.

"We're leaving in ten minutes," Wynn announced, dismissing their comments.

"No coffee?" Brad Colben growled. "I ain't going nowheres without coffee."

"We'll make you coffee," Elsa said.

"Elsa!"

"I need the coffee, Wynn."

Wynn relented. "You're right. But they're not getting any." Curses from the men filled the morning air as she passed Elsa her gun and poured water into a pot from a couple of canteens. She threw in a fistful of grounds she'd found in a cloth sack lying nearby. Soon there was a small fire going, the pot hanging over the flames.

"I gotta take a leak," a man said.

Elsa and Wynn looked at each other.

"Me too," added another. Soon the four outlaws were badgering the women to turn them loose so they could piss.

"We'll help you," Wynn said.

"You ain't touching me, lady." Brad pulled his knees tighter to his body.

"Then piss in your pants."

For all his bravado, the youth looked pained. "Maybe they should be untied for a couple of minutes," Elsa said.

"Free Toss's hands. He'll help them."

"Like hell I will!"

Wynn touched the scar on her cheek put there by his spur. "You did this to me, Toss. I owe you one. Now you help these boys take a leak or I'm gonna take off your spurs and use 'em on your balls."

Wynn was glaring at Baker. She looked as near to shooting him as Elsa herself had been to shooting Sugarfoot last night. Her eyes were as dark as a raccoon's mask. She looked emaciated and weak. She limped so severely that Elsa couldn't understand what kept her upright. Wynn took a threatening step toward Sugarfoot.

Elsa moved toward them. "He'll do it, Wynn. If he won't, I'll just shoot him. I don't like him, anyway."

Wynn stepped back. Her ragged breathing steadied itself. "Right."

Wynn passed Elsa her gun and released Toss's hands. "Get these animals watered," she said. His feet still tightly bound together, he hopped from man to man.

They screamed profanity at the women and at Toss for touching them. A hundred wrathful threats filled the air. The horses pranced and fussed at the screeching, tugging at their ropes. In the end, the men peed where they knelt before Toss tucked them back into their pants. He was the lucky one. He took care of himself before he was bound. And then his cohorts swore at him for being favored by the ladies. He cursed and raged at them and spit in their direction.

The women stood guard, watching for tricks. Elsa wished she could rid herself of the large lump of fear stuck in her throat. Even the blistering coffee couldn't seem to melt it away. She had no idea how much longer she and Wynn could keep each other steady, balanced, going. She could barely recall anymore why she and Wynn were up here in the mountains with four captured and bloodied men. Her ears buzzed; her head buzzed.

The sun was up and brighter than she had ever before witnessed. Even through the dense forest, its glow pierced her awareness. She looked down at her chest. A long golden ray of sun protruded from her bosom. She plucked it out feeling no pain whatsoever. The arrow disintegrated in her hand. "Hey, Wynn, did you see that?" Another ray pierced her hand, passing straight through it. How beautiful. "Wynn, the sun . . ."

The sun's brightness disappeared. A thick cloud passed overhead. Elsa glared at Brad, who was squinting at the blazing host and cursing it, apparently to irritate her. "You made the sun die, Brad Colben. You killed it with your filthy talk." Her eyes glazed as she walked over to Wynn and handed her her gun. "Hold this."

She moved back to Brad and untied his neckerchief from around his throat. She tried to tie it around his face with the bulk of the bandanna across his mouth, but he tossed his head so that she couldn't get the gag in place. He was also trying to bite her.

Infuriated by his lack of cooperation, bad manners and incessant cursing, she said, "You need to keep still." She took a couple of steps backward and knocked him sideways with two vicious kicks in the ribs. "Now sit still and shut up, you slithering viper."

Wynn came over to help, handing Elsa the guns. "Shoot the first thing on him that moves. Fingers, toes, eyes, ears, dick. If it moves, shoot it!"

While Elsa pointed both pistols at Brad, Wynn slapped the bandanna across his mouth, tying it behind his head until he squeezed his eyes shut from the tightening band. But he didn't move otherwise, and he didn't speak.

Taking back her gun, Wynn whirled on the remaining three. "I'll shoot you."

"Take it easy, lady," Toss said. He looked sufficiently scared that she might mean what she said and that she just might pull that trigger. "You keep telling us. We heard you the first time. Don't none of us here want to get shot. You're tough. We see it. Ain't nobody here can't see how tough you are. Right, boys?"

The rest quickly mumbled sincere affirmations.

Wynn stepped close to Toss Baker and screamed into his face. "Then see that you remember. I'm tired and I'm hungry. I want to go home and I don't ever want to look at another goddamn cowboy. Elsa, saddle the horses, and throw the money in one of the saddlebags there."

Elsa dashed about the campground, feeling a little more clearheaded now that she was moving around. She emptied two sets of saddlebags, cramming the money inside both. She chose the largest mount, a skittish bald that pranced about as she threw the blanket and saddle across his back. That done, she secured the bags to the saddle's rear housing and tied them in place with saddle strings. She pushed the bit into the bald's mouth, shoving hard. He threw back his head jerking free of his lead rope and backed twenty feet into the thickets and out of sight with Elsa staying right with him.

"Come on, Elsa," Wynn bellowed. "Hang on to that horse."

A few minutes later Elsa came out of the woods,

leading the horse with fresh scratches on her arms and face.

"What happened?" Wynn's agitation was plain as she moved restlessly in place. "I was about to come looking for you."

Elsa hoisted a second blanket and saddle. "Little trouble with the bridle. It's fine now."

Only two of the four horses were saddled. Wynn drenched the fire with the remaining coffee and kicked dirt over the steaming coals until there was no trace of smoke.

"Who's riding?" Jake asked.

"Not you," she answered. The women rode.

The outlaws' eyes smoldered with rage, their expressions as dangerous as their past deeds had been. Baker's lips drew taut as he emitted something akin to a growl from deep within his throat. Between clenched teeth, he started to speak. "I —"

Elsa pointed her gun at him. "Not a word," she said. She sounded so much braver than she felt. She had passed through the panic stage, most of the nausea stage, the desire-to-run stage and for a moment, a brave stage. But one by one, the old torturous feelings were returning. She mentally repeated Wynn's name over and over and breathed deeply.

The outlaws' feet were freed, but their hands remained tied behind their backs. They walked single file before the mounted women who led the remaining horses burdened with camping gear and food.

The group started down the mountain, picking up Buck on the way. He nickered his pleasure at no longer being deserted.

The brush annoyed Elsa and Wynn far less today since they were clothed and riding horses. The men fared less well, unable to protect their faces from frequent slaps dealt by twigs, and bushes grabbing at their shirts every step of the way. In addition, they were beginning to limp. If there was anything a western man hated it was walking any distance in high-heeled boots specifically designed for the stirrup.

As they rested, the outlaws weren't allowed to sit any closer than eight feet from each other. Elsa relented and removed Brad's gag.

Instantly, he snarled at her. "If I get my hands on you bitches, you'll wish you'd never been born."

"It wouldn't take you to make me feel that way, cowboy," Elsa said. His abuse no longer mattered. He was five hundred dollars on the hoof. That was all he was. He would help save her mama, who was no doubt suffering far more than he ever had.

"I gotta piss," Baker announced.

With his words, the others began protesting.

"Nobody is peeing," Elsa said. As scared as she was, it was time she took more initiative, became more . . . bossy. Mama would probably have slapped somebody by now. It was awful how much she missed Mama. Pretty soon, Mama, she thought. Pretty soon and this'll all be over. I'll see to it.

Wynn gave her a brief smile, lifting Elsa's bitter spirits. Too soon, Wynn said, "Time to go."

Sugarfoot glowered at them. "I ain't moving."

"Okay," Wynn said. "But I'm not leaving you here alive." Her gunshot echoed throughout the woods. The outlaw's hat leaped from his head and rolled a couple of yards away. A hole that hadn't been there a second before had been drilled right through the crown. Wynn was grinning widely, her skin drawn tightly across her cheekbones. "Annie Oakley special."

Elsa jumped along with all the men at the unexpected shot. Their nerves had to be as frayed as hers. And if it were possible, their attitudes were worsening with each passing minute. There were still several days of travel before them. She desperately needed to sleep and something better to eat than the food the men were packing. What a dreadful way to live. "You're all fools," she said.

Someone soundly cursed her, but she didn't care. She was beyond caring about much of anything other than making it back to Wawtauk. Only the thought of the reward money drove her. Without it she and Mama were dead. She mounted up and waved the others to move on. Her ears began buzzing again, and she didn't hear their complaints.

Just before sundown, they stopped for the night. The outlaws were immediately bound hands to feet, behind them. Wynn took care of the horses while Elsa stood guard. That done, Elsa cooked. She threw beans and hardtack into the cook pot, allowing the tasteless food to simmer over a small fire. One at a time the men's hands were released to eat and relieve themselves. Lashed again for the night, their bodies separated from one another by several yards, they settled down to sleep.

A safe distance from them, Elsa and Wynn positioned themselves upright, leaning against two trees growing near each other. Elsa chose the one with a broken twig projecting at just the right height to poke her in the back. She pressed her body against it until she felt a prick. Should she doze and collapse backward or slide down the trunk, the twig would puncture her skin and wake her.

Night sounds increased as the day darkened. Except for their evening fire, the woods would soon be a black unidentifiable creature. Earlier, Elsa had volunteered to gather wood and keep the fire going all night. Anything to help her stay awake.

She listened to the familiar sounds surrounding her. She wasn't as afraid of the noises as she was ten days ago, or was it eleven? She was no longer sure. What she was sure of was that she had sent no money to Mama this past week. She had to avoid thinking about it. Mama must do for herself until Elsa could wire home her reward. The thieves had said fifteen days. It hadn't yet been fifteen days. She still had some time.

Having reassured herself, she listened again to life stirring around her. The leaves were still. There was probably a storm on its way. Lord knew they needed the rain. A nearby rustling alerted her. It came close to her and then receded. "What was that?" she asked Wynn.

"Some animal."

Unconcerned, Elsa closed her eyes and leaned her head against the tree. She counted to three and opened her eyes again. Tomorrow, she thought, she and Wynn *must* work something out. The outlaws weren't going to have to worry about killing them. They were doing a nice job of it all by themselves.

CHAPTER EIGHTEEN

The tempest struck as they began winding their
way down the trail's steepest and roughest terrain
yet. Jutting rocks, slippery roots and slick mud
challenged even the most surefooted of them, human
or horse. The animals slipped dangerously on greasy
earth and rotting foliage, sometimes sliding on their
haunches, their own weight pushing them forward.
The women staunchly stuck to their saddles, pulling
back on the reins, helping the animals maintain their
composure. The packhorses strained at their leads,
but Wynn and Elsa held on tight.

Ahead, the men stumbled, fighting to remain upright. Hands still tied behind their backs, it was a tough job and more than once they fell hard, bruising and cutting themselves and shrieking loud curses at their unfortunate plight. Rapidly, they regained their footing as the horses, wild-eyed and barely controlable, continued bearing down upon them.

For their return trip to Wawtauk, they chose a different course. Originally, the path looked like it was in better condition than the one they had ascended many nights ago. Five miles of relatively easy descent on the remnants of an old logging road convinced them they'd made the right decision.

Then the rain began, but it was too late to turn back. Retracing their steps in the solid downpour would take twice as long and twice the energy that any one of them had left.

As frightening as the downward ride was, Elsa was still grateful for the chilling rain. The cold, pelting drops helped revive her badly dulled senses. Wynn seemed to be in no better shape. She held her injured arm against her body, aching, no doubt, from dampness and cold. Though they both wore sweaters, the garments were useless protection as water ran straight through the woolen material, drenching their cotton dresses beneath.

"I hate this," Wynn screamed into the gale.

Elsa said nothing. Her whole face was stiff with cold, and she hadn't a speck of strength left to reply to useless comments.

She led this morning. If she were to claim half the reward, she religiously believed she should take equal risks, although the men traveling before her were far enough ahead to prevent any surprises.

Their hands remained tied at all times except once in the morning and once each evening as one at a time, they relieved themselves and ate their Spartan meal. Their wrists bled more each day from the chafing ropes.

Despite the bandits' injuries and their frequent yelling, cursing and threats directed at their captors, the women remained dissuaded and cautious. The outlaws were going back to jail, and they were going to collect the reward.

Tall stands of trees hemmed them in on both sides as the party staggered onward. Thunder rolled off the mountains while winds roared and relentless rain beat the exhausted group to numbness. Suddenly these sounds became minor compared to the earth's spontaneous, demonic clamor that welled up to the rear of the small band.

Elsa literally believed the day of judgment had arrived. She spun around in the saddle, fully expecting the great hand of God to come roaring down upon her and slap her off the horse for all her recent cursing and lifelong pettiness.

The rest of the group followed her gaze and then froze. Before their stricken eyes, trees, brush and boulders wrenched themselves free of precarious holds on shallow, water-saturated, mountaintop soil.

The women, the men, even the horses remained transfixed until the bedlam from the massive slide receded. In less than three minutes, the mountain had changed completely, its naked side revealing a vista that would stretch for miles on a clear day.

The avalanche began anew, now occurring before them. The women held their horses' reins so tight, they bruised their mounts' mouths. More falling rocks, trees and soil rolled downward, sounding like a thousand raging bears tearing one another apart. Brad frantically struggled to run from the cascading earth. Had his hands been free, he would easily have made it. Restricted by his bonds, he could do nothing but spin in place at the same rate of speed that the dirt slipped from beneath his feet.

Sugarfoot and Toss scrambled uphill, squatting behind thick tree trunks to avoid Brad's fate.

"Help me, for God's sake," Brad screamed. "Jake, help me."

Jake ran back to Elsa, shouting, "Cut me loose. Cut me loose." He looked at his struggling brother and screamed again, "You can't just let him die like that." His eyes were filled with terror. "Cut me loose, I say."

"No!" Wynn rode up and grabbed Elsa's arm. "Don't even think about it."

Brad was still running in place, the dirt continuing its mad pace to the abyss below, transporting him along with it. His screams were pitiful as he beseeched them for help. "Gimme a rope," he screamed. "Come *on,* somebody. I'm gonna *fall!*"

Elsa pulled away from Wynn. "He's worth five hundred dollars. He goes over the side and we'll lose that money. I'm cutting Jake loose."

"They're *killers!*"

"I'm not." Elsa rapidly dismounted and retrieved a knife from one of the bags.

"Don't do it, Elsa." Wynn stayed in her saddle. "They'll kill us. *You,* get back," she warned Jake.

Elsa paused for a moment.

"Move it, lady," Jake declared frantically. He

looked again at Brad who was being drawn ever closer to the edge.

Elsa gave one more glance at Wynn, then freed the outlaw. He yanked the knife from her grasp, but instead of attacking her or Wynn, he grabbed a rope from Elsa's saddle and ran directly to Brad.

Both brothers ran in place as Jake freed Brad's hands. Rain battered them, and the frightful noise of tumbling earth filled the air. Thunder crashed as lightning struck a nearby tree, its loud crack panicking the already half-crazed horses. Buck's eyes rolled back as he screamed in fear. Held by Wynn's injured hand, he reared, spun to his right and easily ripped the leadrope from her. He tore up the hill, crashing through the woods. He was out of sight before they could stop him.

"Shall I go after him?" Elsa yelled over the rolling thunder.

"No," Wynn shouted. "Let him go. Hang onto the rest."

They swung their attention toward the outlaws. Sugarfoot and Toss were still crouched behind the trees. "Don't you two dare move," Wynn yelled at them.

The remaining horses were close to stampeding as Elsa and Wynn grappled with their leads while attempting to keep their guns pointed at the outlaws. It seemed like they were spread out all over the place, Elsa thought as she guarded the hunched men from her skittish horse and the Colbens still fought for their lives.

As solid rain pummeled them, the earth beneath them all began to shift. Men, women and horses followed the direction Buck had taken, digging hard into the earth that was thinning rapidly beneath their feet. They hit safe ground fifty feet above the precipice and stopped. The Colbens were safe — and free. The knife was still in Jake's possession.

"You women gamble?" he asked. He walked over to Sugarfoot and cut him loose, then pitched the knife to Brad standing near Toss. Casually, Brad cut Toss's bonds.

Elsa drew a bead on Jake. Her hands shook so hard, her thumb slipped off the hammer three times before she could fully cock it.

"I'm a gambling man, ladies," Brad said. "I'm betting we'll lose you in the next ten seconds."

Wynn rode within easy shooting range of them. "I'm betting Elsa and I are gonna shoot you in the next ten seconds," She too had her gun cocked and ready.

"Nah," Brad replied with certainty. "You're meaner'n a den of rattlers, but you ain't killers." Unfettered, the men rubbed life back into their swollen wrists and hands. "I could be wrong, though," Brad said, his voice casual but loud enough for the women to hear him. The storm continued flailing the mountain, and then he slowly raised his hands in surrender before bellowing, "Take off, boys."

That was all the encouragement any of them needed. They split in four different directions, ducking behind brush and trunks and clawing their way over fallen trees.

"They're getting away," Elsa screamed. She fired in their direction. She didn't want to shoot anybody. She only wanted them to come back. Wynn was aiming to hit.

They stopped firing as the trees around them and the fleeing outlaws began sliding downward.

"Look out. Another slide," Sugarfoot shouted fifteen yards to Elsa's right. He leaped and grabbed a tree that skidded right by her as though it weighed nothing. Another dozen trees rumbled past before the earth on which her mount stood began stirring. She dropped the packhorses' leads and spurred her horse hard, driving him upward. Wynn was right beside her. They reached stable ground again and turned around. Several more trees and tons of earth disappeared out of sight. Sugarfoot, his eyes glazed with terror, rode a tree over the edge. His screams rose above the catastrophic din. Seconds later the slide abruptly stopped. As it did, so did the earth's trembling.

The lot of them remained unmoving, paralyzed by the sudden loss of Sugarfoot. Brad stirred first, bolting for the mountain's edge. He fell to his knees, repeating Sugarfoot's name and looked over the edge. A low moan rose from below. "I see him! Christ a'mighty. I can see the son of a bitch."

By then Toss was also kneeling and gawking over the edge. Jake held back, clearly shaken by his own close call.

The women dismounted, holding their horses' reins with death grips while maintaining a prudent distance from the outlaws.

"Throw me a rope," Brad exclaimed, keeping his eyes glued on Sugarfoot. "I can get him out of there."

Wynn tossed her rope toward him.

"Your horse, too."

"No horse," she answered.

"Yours, then," he appealed to Elsa.

"No horse," she replied.

Toss held out his hand. "Then gimme your gun so's I can shoot him. He can't die like this."

Elsa watched the thief and killer for a long time. She dismounted and led the horse toward him, her gun aimed at him every moment. That was five hundred dollars hanging in a tree down there.

Brad fastened the two ropes together, then secured one end to the saddle horn. "Jake, mount up."

Still shaking like a leaf, Jake climbed into the saddle, keeping the horse steady while Brad slid down the rope and over the side, disappearing from view.

Elsa crawled on hands and knees to the mountain's edge. About thirty feet below, Sugarfoot lay draped across a tree branch. The slightest movement would send the whole tangled mess moving downward again.

Brad reached the tree and carefully tied the rope around Sugarfoot's waist. Abruptly, the trunk shifted to an almost upright position. "Pull us up," Brad screamed. Desperation saturated his appeal. "Hurry up. The whole thing's gonna go."

Jake tapped the stallion's sides, yanking back hard on the reins. "Back, back, boy." Toss walked backward before the horse, keeping a hand on the animal's neck, talking softly to him.

The rope tied to the horn grew taut as horse and rider withdrew inches at a time. "Keep going," came a desperate yell from below.

The stallion backed several more yards. Elsa watched as Sugarfoot barely clung to Brad who supported his full weight around the waist, the rope sustaining them both.

The dangling men were within five feet of the top when the rope snapped. Screams and sounds of bodies crashing through the trees below filled the air. Then it was still. Even the thunder and pelting rain had stopped.

"Oh, my God," Elsa whispered. She still gaped at the space where the men had fallen through. "Oh, my God."

Wynn whipped around. "Get off," she commanded Jake. "Toss, you move away. We're not losing you too."

Jake dismounted slowly, an ugly look crossing his face, tightening his skin. "That was my brother!" he screamed. He aged before Elsa's eyes as his hair dripped rivulets of water down his face. His shoulders slumped and his fingers opened and closed, opened and closed. It seemed that in the last ten minutes, his voice had deepened to full manhood. He took a step away from the horse. "All I am to you is nothing but a goddamn reward, ain't I? You don't even give a shit about those two men who just died." His voice dropped to a whisper. "You goddamn witches. I'm gonna kill you."

Wynn cocked her gun. "I've been beat up by better horses than you, asshole. So *get moving*." Her voice rose. Tears filled her eyes and coursed down her cheeks. She took a menacing step in the direction of the man moving closer and closer to her like a cat stalking prey.

Jake snarled viciously, low and threatening. He bared his teeth as he clenched his hands, shaping his fingers into claws formed to choke a throat.

Elsa grabbed the barrel of her gun and ran toward Jake. "Stop. Stop it, you two." The space between the two adversaries shrank. "Stop it, I say." Elsa walked within two feet of Jake. He seemed unaware that she was near him. She raised the gun by the barrel and struck him over the head. The handle split his scalp and blood gushed over his face. He dropped to his knees from the blow and fell sideways.

Wynn stared with uncomprehending eyes at the downed man before her. Elsa positioned herself between the outlandish rivals, one a thief and murderer, the other a trick rider whose greatest talent lay in riding any way but upright on a galloping horse.

Elsa looked deep into her eyes. "You too, Wynn," she said. "It's time to stop."

Wynn's weaponed hand dropped to her side. "I'd have killed him."

"We don't need to," Elsa said. "I'll tie him up. We'll drag him off this mountain if we have to, but he's going back with us alive." She looked around. "Where's Toss?" Toss had obviously taken advantage of the fracas and run. "He's gotta be right around here," she said. "I'll go after him. Five hundred —"

"Damn it, Elsa. Forget the money for once. Let's just get off this cursed mountain."

"He can't be far. We've got horses."

"*Forget it*! He'd jump you and kill you before you knew he was there."

While Elsa waited in sullen silence, Wynn tied Jake's wrists behind his back and then bound the rope to his feet. He didn't try to fight her. Blood draining into his eyes blinded him. The blow to his head made him sluggish. He was no longer a threat, now, only a hideous-looking, evil young man.

Confident he couldn't escape, she came back to Elsa and sat beside her.

Elsa asked, "Do you think Toss'll come back?"

"Yes, but he'll wait until we're careless."

"That isn't going to happen again. You sleep. I'll watch. Then we'll switch."

Wynn nodded. For the rest of the night the former department store worker maintained vigil over the former show girl and the current outlaw as they both lay open-mouthed and unconscious with sleep. By the grace of God, Toss was apparently still running from them.

It rained off and on throughout the night. The two remaining horses stood with heads drooping, their riders oblivious to the damp and the fog obscuring anything beyond twenty feet away. The tiny circle of life remained undisturbed until dawn, Elsa choosing to stay awake throughout the night. Wynn was just too whipped to make decent speed tomorrow without some rest.

As the day grew light, the sun burned away thick, gray clouds.

Elsa rubbed stubborn grittiness from her eyes. She longed for the city she had left behind, with its noisy drays and wagons, hawkers populating her street, children running about and neighbors that she could talk to if she chose, without having to walk twenty-five miles before laying eyes on another rational human being.

She nudged Wynn with her shoe. "Time to move." Her throat was scratchy and sore.

Wynn awoke, unwinding slowly, loosening her

joints and the cricks in her neck, emitting little moans as she moved.

Elsa checked on Jake, still dead asleep. The blood on his scalp and face had been washed away by the night's rain. He didn't appear half as scary as he had the evening before, but he looked just as deadly. Elsa shuddered and returned to Wynn's side.

She longed to lean over and kiss Wynn's neck that lay exposed to the warming sun. She was about to put her desire into motion when Jake stirred. "I'm dyin'," he said. "Turn me loose. My hands are gonna fall off."

Elsa ignored him. "Come on, Wynn. We've got to get going."

Wynn opened one eye at a time. "What time is it?" She sat hunched over, her hair hanging in a tangled mess around her face. She was plastered with dirt and needles just as Elsa was. Their clothing was barely useful enough to get them back to town in modest fashion. "The sun's up."

"Probably about five-thirty."

"How's he?" Wynn moved stiffly, nodding in Jake's general direction.

"Unhappy."

"Too bad."

Elsa agreed. He would stay tied until delivered.

Their prisoner saw the women stirring. "I gotta piss," he yelled. "Turn me loose."

Wynn walked over to Jake and squatted beside him. "I'll help you, or you'll suffer. What'll it be?"

He suffered with humiliation as Wynn assisted him and then moved away.

"It's a goddamn *sin*," he screamed at them, "the way you treat a man. A *sin!*"

"So's killing," Wynn said. She rinsed her hands in a pool of water that had collected in a shallow dip at the base of a tree. She repeated the process twice more, then shook them dry. "God, he stinks. Let's skip a fire and just eat cold beans."

"I ain't killed nobody," Jake growled.

"Not in the past few days, you haven't," Elsa agreed.

"You never will again, either," Wynn said. "I promise."

Elsa felt suddenly filled with uninhibited hate. "I loath men like you, Colben," she said. "I'll be glad to take the money for bringing you in." She walked away and looked at the eastern valley miles below them. She was still angry with her father, but she would feel that his death would be vindicated if this man hanged. He wasn't Papa's killer, but he was a killer all the same. Any executed murderer would do.

They made their way eastward for two more days, the mountains demanding that they climb up and then down before descending lower and lower to the foothills.

Each morning after Wynn helped Jake relieve himself, he grappled to his feet, saying, "You bitches will never take me in." He swayed back and forth, his eyes feverish and bloodshot. His sparse beard was laced with debris from the forest floor and his clothing was mud-covered and smelling of a strong male odor. Once rid of him, Elsa would never get this close to a man again. She didn't hate men. She

205

just didn't like what they became once they stepped beyond being human.

At ten o'clock, they took a rest. Elsa looked around her. "You know, Wynn, I thought for sure we'd reach treeline by now."

Wynn considered Elsa's words. "That's what I've been thinking. It can't be that much farther."

Jake backed up to a rock and slid down its side until he rested on the ground. He threw back his head and laughed as though he had just heard the funniest joke in the world.

Elsa snapped, "What's wrong with you?"

"You're lost, ain't you? Lost!" He roared louder, amused beyond reason.

"He's just going nuts, that's all," Wynn said. "We're not lost."

"Yeah, you are," he corrected. "I knew that yesterday. You'll never take me, you dumb . . ." He was laughing so hard that tears ran down his face, streaking the dirt on his furry cheeks, carrying away muddy droplets and dumping them onto his chest.

Elsa slid from her saddle and sat on a fallen log. She fiddled with the reins of her horse. Wynn collapsed beside her.

"You're lost, ladies," Jake happily yelled.

It was clear that Wynn's temper was rising like the morning sun. Elsa shook her head, indicating that Wynn should ignore him.

"Well, that takes care of this little trip, don't it?" Again he was hollering.

Wynn looked his way. "Is that all you can do is yell your stupid head off? Shut up."

In mock fear, Jake drew back. "Now that's scary, Wynn. I'm scared to death. You ain't gonna shoot me. You ain't gonna do nothin' to me. You ain't even gonna take me in."

"You're going in, friend," Elsa said. "If we have to drag you, you're going in."

He laughed resoundingly. "Not by you two bitches."

He was right about that. Silenced by a strong hand clamped over her mouth, Elsa was pulled backward off the log. A fist struck her head, stunning her. When she came to, she found herself tightly bound, her hands behind her back.

She opened her mouth to scream, but she was silenced by a neckerchief. She could taste sweat and smell its terrible odor. She began retching, bile welling up in her throat as panic built within her. She'd choke to death if she didn't stop. Fighting to swallow while spitting around the bandanna, she blew vomit out through her nostrils and at the sides of her mouth. With eyes watering from turbulent spasms, she brought her heaving guts under control.

Wynn lay on the ground a few feet from Elsa. She had also been bound and gagged, her eyes glaring at four men with a fury that could have set the trees on fire.

"Kill them right now," Toss said. The gunmen sat side by side on the log Elsa and Wynn had recently occupied. Brad and Sugarfoot were black and blue wherever their skin was exposed. Deep gashes split their faces in several places. They'd lost their hats and their hair was thickly matted with blood.

"Okay by me. I get to shoot 'em both," Jake said. "Look at my goddamn hands. They're never gonna work right again."

"Go ahead," Toss answered. "Then let's get the hell out of here. We're too damned close to town."

"I know what you're thinking, ladies," Brad said, chuckling wickedly. "We should have died back there."

"I prayed like hell all the way down the mountain that we wouldn't," Sugarfoot answered. "Hell of a ride, weren't it, Brad?" He too seemed amused beyond sensibility. "Never had a prayer work before. Maybe I'll become a preacher."

Elsa surmised that she and Wynn hadn't been off the trail after all. And all that loud yelling and laughter Jake executed was a cover for any sounds the others might have made until they were in position to grab her and Wynn. She wondered how long they'd been tailed.

Jake pointed the guns at Elsa and Wynn. "Things sure have changed, ain't they, ladies?"

Elsa studied the weapons and the bandits. So it was over for her and for Wynn. She was going to die right there on the side of some nameless mountain she had no business being on, had it not been for Papa.

Surrounded by the threatening demons about to end her life, she wasn't afraid. Miss Ashley came to mind. Elsa used to be so scared of her. She laughed grimly through the bandanna at the thought of it.

"Shut up, bitch," Jake yelled. He slapped her across the head, rocking her sideways.

She sat up again, not caring that she'd been struck. There were worse things in life than physical pain. There was the pain of failing completely. She'd also never been a very good clerk or friend or daughter. She'd just sort of passed through each day's hours, every day, through the years until she'd reached this moment in time. Here it would all end.

Soon it would end for Mama, too. Elsa wasn't able to save her own mother. She was a gambler, no better than Papa. She was going to die just like he had.

Wynn stared at the men, displaying no fear of their power over her or the weapons leveled at her. She grunted something incoherent while looking intensely at Elsa.

Elsa read the devotion in her eyes. Oh, how much she loved this woman. She rose to her knees still keeping her eyes on Wynn and started toward her. She wanted to be near Wynn when they died.

Brad moved in and kicked her sideways. "Stay there, bitch. You'll get to watch all right."

Elsa's eyes didn't move. She continued watching and again got to her knees, determined that she and Wynn would die side by side. They would, they would, they would.

This time Brad let her be. Along the way, she sliced her knee on a sharp rock. The gash bled profusely. Reaching Wynn's side, Wynn looked at her bleeding knee. Elsa shrugged off the injury. Soon she would have a bullet hole in her. That wound would matter.

She sat solidly next to Wynn, close enough so that they touched. They maintained eye contact with each other.

"Bet if I put this gun right here," Jake said, pressing the barrel against Elsa's temple, "the bullet would go clear through old Wynn's head, too." He leaned into Wynn's face. "What do you think, little darlin'?"

Wynn kept her eyes focused on Elsa's.

"Try it," Sugarfoot goaded. He patted the bulging saddle bags still tied to Elsa's mount. "Bet you half your take it don't work."

"You're on," Jake said.

He thumbed back the hammer, the noise reverberating loudly against Elsa's skull. She kept Wynn in focus as well as she could. Wynn was also still with her. She felt Wynn lean against her just a little harder. Elsa nodded that it was all right for Jake to shoot now. She was ready to die.

CHAPTER NINETEEN

"Over this way." A shout split the wooded silence. "No, it was over here. I saw it last year."

Children's voices! Then came the sound of a man's voice. "Watch where you walk. There're snakes around here and all kinds of poison plants."

Elsa looked toward the sound. The minister! There must be a drive and a hike going on. They were awfully far from Wawtauk.

Jake still held the gun pressed against Elsa's skull. She was willing to die because she had no choice, but killing children was beyond her tolerance, and she knew these men wouldn't hesitate at shooting a child if they could so easily run down a woman in the street, slap her around and gleefully shoot her dead.

She threw herself forward, screaming through her gag and thrashing around like a body gone berserk.

The men jumped back to escape her flailing legs.

Wynn took her cue, kicking and grunting, working her way toward anybody close to her. She lashed out with her feet and caught Sugarfoot in the crotch.

Brad clamped his hand over Sugarfoot's mouth before he could howl. "Get the goddamn horses and ride," he hissed.

Jake followed Elsa's thrashing head movements with his pistol. "I'm gonna kill these —"

Brad shoved Sugarfoot toward the horses and then hit his brother so hard he fell like a sack of feed. He picked him up and slung him over a saddle.

"Check the moneybags," Sugarfoot said.

"They're okay," Jake moaned. "I been watching them for days. Now lemme off this horse."

Sugarfoot rode alone while Brad rode double with his half-conscious brother still hanging across the saddle. They galloped away from the town, away from the children, away from the women who, still bound and gagged, continued kicking and grunting desperately, trying to draw the hikers' attention.

"Get back," the minister shouted. "Come this way, William. *William!* It sounds like a big animal. Come on, we've got to get out of here. Bear, children, bear! Quickly, come on, now."

The women kicked and screamed even more. Elsa listened to the children and the preacher climbing into buggies and rushing down the mountain.

Elsa lay exhausted and disheartened. The screaming voices faded as the hikers scurried back to town.

Except for the birds that had again taken up their song since the ruckus had ceased, the forest was quiet. The outlaws were probably already a couple of miles away. Elsa doubted they'd be back. Not with people so close by and their faces plastered on posters all over the territory. And, too, they had the saddlebags.

She and Wynn got to their feet. Wynn looked dreadful, but Elsa saw instead a beautiful woman more precious to her than anything else in the world, more dear than the reward or her own life. They tipped their faces toward each other until their foreheads touched. Wynn's skin was gritty with dirt and wet with sweat. Yet Elsa couldn't remember a more wonderful feeling than that small area of Wynn's soiled face touching her own. The gag prevented her from speaking clearly, but she managed to mumble through the foul bandanna, "I love you, Wynn." It sounded more like, "Ahhhuuuuvvvvvv."

Wynn's eyes twinkled as she replied, "Haaaaaa-vaaa." She moved around to Elsa's back so that Elsa could free her hands. Elsa's fingers were so numb from the rawhide thong that she could barely move them, let alone feel anything with them. It took her nearly an hour to release Wynn. Meanwhile, she chewed her way through the vile neckerchief binding her mouth. She gagged and threw up nothing and gagged and vomited more. Finally, her stomach was satisfied. Her entire body ached.

Wynn ripped away her gag as well, spitting and then conjuring up more saliva so that she could spit again. While cleansing her mouth of any remnants of the rag, she freed Elsa's hands.

Elsa said, "I don't ever want to put anything in my mouth again."

They sank breathless and exhausted to the earth. "Are you sure?" Wynn asked. She rested her head against a drawn knee.

"I'm sure."

Wynn smiled at her. "Flex your hands, move your fingers. Get your blood circulating again."

Except for their intense hunger and exhaustion and the fact that they didn't think they were more than twenty miles from town, they were jubilant. They couldn't actually dance, but they managed a weak hug, one that held them up. Assured they were fine, Elsa said, "I'm going after those men."

Wynn attempted to speak several times, but only bits of words and sounds came out of her mouth. She finally managed to say, "Are you *crazy*?"

Elsa felt mean. "Those men are mine. One of the horses is mine. The reward is mine. They owe me."

"We're not going after them, Elsa."

"What day is it? Have you been keeping track of the days?"

Wynn shook her head.

"I have," Elsa said, feeling primal. "If I've kept track right, in two days my mama is going to be killed unless I wire her enough money. I'm going after them. I'm walking out of here today and getting another horse and going after those killers. They murdered my papa."

Wynn grabbed Elsa's arm. "*They* did not kill your father, Elsa. Somebody else did. One man did. Not three. And not these three. Use your head. You did your best."

"They're mine."

Staggering and falling, weak with fatigue, starvation and thirst, Elsa started down the mountain. The streams had given out two miles ago. She drew herself up and fell again. Spots of light flashed before her eyes. Wynn, in no better shape, grasped branches and bushes, following Elsa down the mountain.

They made eight tortuous miles that day and then staggered on through the night until they could move no more, sleeping until dawn. Neither knew a thing about what was safe to eat from the land, and so they chewed on prairie grass and spit it out. It gave their mouths something to do.

The following morning, Wawtauk shimmered in the distance from the sun's intense heat. They had reached the road they started up a lifetime ago. "I need to get to that telegraph office today, Wynn."

Wynn looked at her. Her eyes were nearly swollen shut from too much sun and vicious bites by bugs that lived well at this much lower elevation. Her face, arms and legs were laced with multiple cuts and bruises. The dress she wore was no longer fit to be a good rag. I look just like that, Elsa thought. Like a wild animal. "Those men are mine," she said.

"You're crazy, Elsa," Wynn said. "We need to get some food and water into us before we think about going after them again. We haven't seen a stream since yesterday."

"I thought you hated the idea."

"If you go, I'll have to."

"Right now I have to get to that telegraph office. What time does it close?"

"Five. At least that's what I remember."

"Mama will hear today that I'm still trying. I'm gonna win, Wynn." She laughed hysterically.

Wynn clearly saw nothing funny.

They began their final trek, swaying as though drunk.

A horse galloped up behind them creating a swirl of dust as the horse halted. Lethargically, Elsa turned to see who it was. A horse could get them to town.

Sugarfoot glared at them. He hurled two pairs of saddle bags to the ground. They landed at Elsa's feet. He leaped from his horse and grabbed her by the shoulders. He shook her, and in her weakened condition, she flopped like a rag doll. He slapped her, screaming in her face, "Where is it?"

Wynn flew into the outlaw. "Leave her alone," she yelled. She barely moved him. He backhanded her, and she fell as though she weighed nothing.

"Where is it?" he said again. Elsa dropped to the ground as he released her.

"You have your money, if that's what you're looking for."

He kicked her in the ribs, knocking her breathless. Wynn fought her way up to attack him again. She was completely powerless as once more he repelled her with a mighty shove that lifted her off her feet and sent her reeling. She landed on her back, her lungs emptying in a long heave.

"Leave her be," Elsa gasped. The bandit came over to kneel before her. He grabbed her hair and pulled her face into his. "You got that money, bitch. Where'd you hide it?"

"I didn't take it," she said. "Ask Jake. He can tell you. He was with us a lot of days you and Brad weren't. You don't know everything that happened."

"What happened? *What?*"

"Ask him. Ask him where the flat-top rock is. It's right near where you found us."

Sugarfoot's eyes belayed deep distrust. "You're lying."

"Why would I even bother? You can shoot me anytime you want."

"I'll be back before you reach town. I set this job up myself, and I ain't carrying no empty saddlebags for nothing. If Jake took it, he's dead. If you took it, I won't kill you. You'll live until you tell me where it is, because right over there is the thing that's gonna make you talk."

He gestured to Wynn.

"Ask Jake," Elsa said.

He gave her a vicious slap before remounting. From the saddle, he surveyed them. "Somebody's gonna die before this day is finished." He whirled and savagely spurred his mount. When the dust settled, he was a tiny being just disappearing into the tree line.

Elsa scrambled over to Wynn. She was breathing but unconscious. "Oh, Wynn," she said fervently. "I hate this place. I *hate* it. Wake up, precious darling. Please wake up." She fanned Wynn with her skirt until she came to and then shaded her face from the hot sun until she had recovered.

Wynn clutched her hands against her chest. "Is he gone?"

"He's gone."

"He'll be back."

"Not before we reach town."

"He'll kill you — us — for stealing the money. You lied to him, and now you're lying to me. I haven't been paying a lick of attention to you other than to see that you're all right. That flat chest of yours. You're bigger. You've been carrying that money for days. Is that why it took you so long to get that bridle on the bald? You were stuffing your clothes back there in the woods." Wynn shook with anger. "We were free of them. How long do you think it'll take Sugarfoot to figure out the truth?"

Elsa squinted against the sun as she calculated their distance. "We have twelve miles to go. Sugarfoot has sixteen, roundtrip. We can beat him."

Wynn said disgustedly, "I bet we can crawl there at two inches an hour." She spat and moved on.

"Mama . . ."

"Yeah, yeah, I know."

The sun beat down on them, and bugs attacked them. Elsa's thirst became a raging thing as Sugarfoot loomed in her mind. She frequently looked over her shoulder, expecting him at any moment as his threat pushed her to her limits.

Elsa recalled going cold with terror as she rammed the money into her clothing and stuffed the bags with dead leaves. She had been smart to keep her mouth shut. Wynn would be dead now if she hadn't.

They stumbled and fell countless times, each pulling the other back to her feet, then continuing on. By four-thirty, they reached Wawtauk. Elsa looked back once more. The road was clear. They had beaten him.

"We win," she said to Wynn.

"We win," Wynn repeated. She smiled through a thick coating of dust.

Someone said, "What in the world?" Somehow Elsa was looking up at a woman. She realized she was lying on her back in the road. Hands picked her up and began carrying her off.

Wynn appeared at her side. "Leave her to me. She'll be fine."

A small crowd gathered around them, wanting to help the poor ladies, one limping pitifully, the other barely able to stand. The townswomen reached out with tentative hands. Wynn refused their help. "We'll be fine. We're just a little tired."

Wynn sunk to her knees. A man grabbed her and righted her. "Where are you headed, ladies? Let me help you."

"The bank," Elsa whispered. "I've got to get to the bank before it closes."

"Why, ma'am, the bank closes at two o'clock, same as always."

Both Elsa and Wynn shoved everyone from their path and headed on rubbery legs toward the bank. "Then open it," Elsa commanded. "I've got the money that was stolen."

CHAPTER TWENTY

Dozens of townspeople crowded into the bank to see the two Eastern women who, singlehandedly, had recovered the bank's money. George Springer, the handsome, thin banker whose face glowed joyously had given his office over to Elsa and Wynn. The office had a modest desk and black leather chair with two more nearby. The papered walls of pale yellow displayed the bank's original sign, repaired and placed in the office as a memento to the old building. A tan leather couch took up the left wall. The office was built by the people for the people. They had kept it simple but functional.

Elsa slipped out of her clothing. Hundred-dollar bills fell to the floor. Many remained plastered against her skin. Wynn helped Elsa peel off the money while just beyond the locked door, Mr. Springer himself stood guard. Two additional men remained outside to make sure that the outlaws didn't suddenly come tearing down the street and start shooting up the town.

"You did a brave thing, Elsa," Wynn said. "You've always wondered about your bravery, haven't you?"

"Cowardliness . . ."

"No, bravery." Wynn striped several more bills from Elsa's back. "Cowardice doesn't suit you at all."

Elsa was fidgety. "We need to hurry. That telegraph office is supposed to close . . ." She glanced at a wall clock loudly ticking her mother's life away. ". . . in ten minutes."

They clawed the rest of the money off Elsa's body. Bills were glued to her back, fanny and thighs where they had been stuffed into her underwear. Elsa had also managed to tuck several hundred dollars into her shoes.

The whole process took only a couple of minutes. The delay would be in counting it.

Wynn scooped up the bills while Elsa pulled on her rags. "That was all the money there was in the sacks," Elsa said. She tugged on her shoes. "I hope to hell it's all there. I wouldn't want to fall under suspicion."

Wynn set the final pile on Stringer's desk as Elsa flung open the door. Oohs and ahs could be heard by

221

those able to peek around Springer's lanky frame at the piles of cash on the desk.

"Count it," Wynn commanded.

He smiled patiently at her. "Of course."

"Now! I'm in a real big hurry." Elsa pulled him inside and slammed the door.

Springer sat at his desk and began the count. Elsa wanted to tear out her hair. This man's slender fingered hands were driving her nuts. The clock read 4:55. "I need my reward now. *Right* now!"

Wynn leaned across his desk and very close to his face. "How about if we help you count it?"

Elsa leaned with her. "I'm a former clerk in a large department store in New York. I'm as qualified as you to tally this cash." Her head was spinning wildly. She clutched the edges of the desk so that she wouldn't faint and tipped her head back as far as she could. She'd heard somewhere that this was a good way to prevent swooning. She stood upright, her head still tipped. The dizziness left her and again she leaned forward. "Let us help."

"All done," he said.

Elsa looked dazed. "All done?"

"While you rested on the couch."

"I don't remember resting on any couch." But there she lay.

Wynn was close by her side. "You fainted a couple of minutes ago."

The clock began to strike, each gong drawing Mama closer and closer to her death. Elsa suspected Mama had been waiting daily at the telegraph office for some word, some money, *something* from her daughter. Elsa needed to send the reward now. Right now!

"Eighty thousand dollars. It's all there, ladies. They never had a chance to spend a dollar of it." Grinning happily, Springer looked as though he could burst.

"The reward," Elsa said, sitting up quickly. Her head reeled again.

"Right here," Mr. Springer handed her a prepared check.

Her eyes widened and her head grew fuzzy as she read: $10,000.00.

Wynn yanked Elsa to her feet and swung her around. They both nearly fell to the floor. They had no energy left, barely enough to cry.

"But . . . but . . . I'm too late," Elsa cried. She collapsed on the couch. "I'm too late!"

With considerable effort, Wynn dragged Elsa to her feet. "You're not too late."

"But the clock."

"Maybe the one in New York is slow," Wynn said hopefully.

"Actually," Mr. Springer informed them, "New York City telegraph offices are open twenty-four hours a day."

"Does that include Staten Island?"

"I believe so," Springer said. "I'm quite sure that it does."

Elsa choked. "Then there's still time." She broke out in loud sobs.

Wynn took Elsa into her arms and held her, rocking her as she would a child. "We have time now, Elsa. We can take care of things now, and take care of each other."

"Could you rewrite the check into equal halves, Mr. Springer?" Elsa asked in broken sobs. "Wynn, here, gets half."

As he did, he said, "The town will certainly remember you, ladies. My, my, my. What will women be doing next? You ladies are going to be our heroines. We'll have a big picnic. There could be a band . . ."

Limping and leaning on each other, Elsa and Wynn left him midspeech, passed through the admiring crowd and headed directly to the telegraph office.

Elsa sent her entire reward to Mama, holding nothing back for herself.

"My turn." Wynn wired Elsa's mother another two thousand.

"Wynn!"

"It was worth the adventure. What's left is ours. We'll pay for the buggy and for Buck if he didn't come back." She smiled and pocketed the difference.

"I'll pay you back."

"No, Elsa, you won't. This deal is done, finished. I got what I wanted out of it, and so did you. I'm not poor anymore, and you're out from under your father's debt. Let's call the whole thing closed."

"But two thousand dollars. If we could have brought back those men . . ."

"But we didn't. So, let's go get something to eat, buy some new clothes and see if Mrs. Kettle will give us a room."

"Mama will faint with shock," Elsa said.

"You look like hell, you know that?"

"You too."

"Food and then bed."

"Bath, too. Why don't we try Mrs. Kettle first? She may forgive us."

No matter where they laid their heads that night, she and Wynn would sleep without fear. Elsa wouldn't even bother having a dream. Not even a good one.

Indeed, Mrs. Kettle did forgive and welcome back the women. She fed them broth and thick slices of bread and cold milk from the cellar's vat. She took it upon herself to move the galvanized tub into their room, keeping it filled with hot water while first Elsa then Wynn soaked away dirt and grime and cleansed their numberless wounds.

Mrs. Kettle provided them with thick, flannel nightgowns. "You can buy clothes tomorrow, ladies. Tonight, just rest. I'm proud to have you in my house. I feel much safer with you here, just knowing what you can do. My goodness, heroines right in my own house." She turned down their covers and fluffed their pillows. "Now, you ladies sleep as late as you like. No one will disturb you." Thumbing her chest, she said, "I'll see to it." She left them alone to slip into their nightgowns.

Elsa was in bed and asleep so fast that she barely even felt Wynn climb in alongside her and fasten her arm around her, saying, "Now I can hold you, my darling." Seconds later they were asleep.

The following day, they awoke very late. If the

clock was correct, it was nearing suppertime. Elsa went over to the window, massaging her eyes. "I've never been so tired in my life."

Wynn mumbled something in return.

Elsa looked through the curtains, her attention riveted on a man riding into town. "Wynn, get up."

"Later."

Elsa hurried to Wynn and yanked the blankets onto the floor. "*Now.*"

Wynn snarled her displeasure.

"Go look out the window."

Wynn dragged herself from bed and pulled back the curtain. The bounty hunter, looking disheveled as ever, led four horses, each with a man's body draped across the saddle.

"That's my money down there," Elsa said, speaking as though she owned the dead outlaws. "I got them close enough to town to get caught."

"*We* got them close enough to town," Wynn corrected. "I was there too, remember?"

"That money rightfully belongs to us," Elsa hissed angrily.

Wynn sat on the chair and gave a weary sigh. "Elsa, we're lucky we're alive. We were just plain lucky all the way through." She rested her elbows on her knees and stared at the floor. "We were as crazy as those killers to even think we could catch them. Dumb luck, that's all it was, just plain dumb luck."

"We should have gotten that money, too."

"*God almighty.*" Wynn walked over to the bed and climbed back under the covers. "Money isn't everything, Elsa. But now and then people get lucky and get what they need. You got what you came here for. I got enough to live on for a while. Maybe even enough to get somebody to take a look at my arm and fix the damned thing and get a thicker sole put on one shoe so I can quit this blamed limping. So let's call it good." Her voice fell to a low warning timbre. "You got your daddy's gambling blood in you, Elsa. You win, you want to play again. You'll lose next time. Gamblers always lose eventually. They lose everything. Everything and everyone." She punched up her pillow and settled down. "I need to sleep right now. Then I want to go home."

Elsa's heart pounded. To lose Wynn was inconceivable. "Where's home?"

"Staten Island. It's far from Mother. You should go home too."

"I want to."

"Do you?"

"You're right, Wynn. I do seem to be like Papa. That's a scary thing. It killed him. Darn near killed us." Elsa's eyes drifted out of focus. "Always looking for the one big chance that would fix all his financial troubles. A little piece of lead not much bigger than my fingernail took care of them for him." She turned from the window. "Papa's debt is settled." She nodded to herself. "That's enough."

Climbing in beside Wynn, she said, "When we get back there, I'm telling Mama that you'll be staying with us."

"She doesn't like show people, remember?"

"She doesn't like being alone either. Do you think you could stand living with her for a while? We could look for an apartment."

"I think that'd be just fine," Wynn said. "She'll just have to gamble that I'm not a danger to her or to you. She'll win, of course."

"Of course."

They wrapped their arms tightly around each other and kissed, a soft long kiss.

A few of the publications of
THE NAIAD PRESS, INC.
P.O. Box 10543 • Tallahassee, Florida 32302
Phone (904) 539-5965
Toll-Free Order Number: 1-800-533-1973
Mail orders welcome. Please include 15% postage.
Write or call for our free catalog which also features an
incredible selection of lesbian videos.

COSTA BRAVA by Marta Balletbo Coll. 144 pp. Read the book, see the movie! ISBN 1-56280-153-8 $11.95

MEETING MAGDALENE & OTHER STORIES by Marilyn Freeman. 160 pp. Read the book, see the movie! ISBN 1-56280-170-8   11.95

SECOND FIDDLE by Kate Calloway. 240 pp. P.I. Cassidy James' second case. ISBN 1-56280-169-6   11.95

LAUREL by Isabel Miller. 128 pp. By the author of the beloved *Patience and Sarah*. ISBN 1-56280-146-5   10.95

LOVE OR MONEY by Jackie Calhoun. 240 pp. The romance of real life. ISBN 1-56280-147-3   10.95

SMOKE AND MIRRORS by Pat Welch. 224 pp. 5th Helen Black Mystery. ISBN 1-56280-143-0   10.95

DANCING IN THE DARK edited by Barbara Grier & Christine Cassidy. 272 pp. Erotic love stories by Naiad Press authors. ISBN 1-56280-144-9   14.95

TIME AND TIME AGAIN by Catherine Ennis. 176 pp. Passionate love affair. ISBN 1-56280-145-7   10.95

PAXTON COURT by Diane Salvatore. 256 pp. Erotic and wickedly funny contemporary tale about the business of learning to live together. ISBN 1-56280-114-7   10.95

INNER CIRCLE by Claire McNab. 208 pp. 8th Carol Ashton Mystery. ISBN 1-56280-135-X   10.95

LESBIAN SEX: AN ORAL HISTORY by Susan Johnson. 240 pp. Need we say more? ISBN 1-56280-142-2   14.95

BABY, IT'S COLD by Jaye Maiman. 256 pp. 5th Robin Miller Mystery. ISBN 1-56280-141-4   19.95

WILD THINGS by Karin Kallmaker. 240 pp. By the undisputed mistress of lesbian romance. ISBN 1-56280-139-2   10.95

THE GIRL NEXT DOOR by Mindy Kaplan. 208 pp. Just what you'd expect. ISBN 1-56280-140-6   10.95

NOW AND THEN by Penny Hayes. 240 pp. Romance on the westward journey. ISBN 1-56280-121-X   10.95

HEART ON FIRE by Diana Simmonds. 176 pp. The romantic and erotic rival of *Curious Wine*. ISBN 1-56280-152-X   10.95

DEATH AT LAVENDER BAY by Lauren Wright Douglas. 208 pp. 1st Allison O'Neil Mystery. ISBN 1-56280-085-X   10.95

YES I SAID YES I WILL by Judith McDaniel. 272 pp. Hot romance by famous author. ISBN 1-56280-138-4   10.95

FORBIDDEN FIRES by Margaret C. Anderson. Edited by Mathilda Hills. 176 pp. Famous author's "unpublished" Lesbian romance. ISBN 1-56280-123-6   21.95

SIDE TRACKS by Teresa Stores. 160 pp. Gender-bending Lesbians on the road. ISBN 1-56280-122-8   10.95

HOODED MURDER by Annette Van Dyke. 176 pp. 1st Jessie Batelle Mystery. ISBN 1-56280-134-1   10.95

WILDWOOD FLOWERS by Julia Watts. 208 pp. Hilarious and heart-warming tale of true love. ISBN 1-56280-127-9   10.95

NEVER SAY NEVER by Linda Hill. 224 pp. Rule #1: Never get involved with . . . ISBN 1-56280-126-0   10.95

THE SEARCH by Melanie McAllester. 240 pp. Exciting top cop Tenny Mendoza case. ISBN 1-56280-150-3   10.95

THE WISH LIST by Saxon Bennett. 192 pp. Romance through the years. ISBN 1-56280-125-2   10.95

FIRST IMPRESSIONS by Kate Calloway. 208 pp. P.I. Cassidy James' first case. ISBN 1-56280-133-3   10.95

OUT OF THE NIGHT by Kris Bruyer. 192 pp. Spine-tingling thriller. ISBN 1-56280-120-1   10.95

NORTHERN BLUE by Tracey Richardson. 224 pp. Police recruits Miki & Miranda — passion in the line of fire. ISBN 1-56280-118-X   10.95

LOVE'S HARVEST by Peggy J. Herring. 176 pp. by the author of *Once More With Feeling*. ISBN 1-56280-117-1   10.95

THE COLOR OF WINTER by Lisa Shapiro. 208 pp. Romantic love beyond your wildest dreams. ISBN 1-56280-116-3   10.95

FAMILY SECRETS by Laura DeHart Young. 208 pp. Enthralling romance and suspense. ISBN 1-56280-119-8   10.95

INLAND PASSAGE by Jane Rule. 288 pp. Tales exploring conventional & unconventional relationships. ISBN 0-930044-56-8   10.95

DOUBLE BLUFF by Claire McNab. 208 pp. 7th Carol Ashton Mystery. ISBN 1-56280-096-5   10.95

BAR GIRLS by Lauran Hoffman. 176 pp. See the movie, read the book! ISBN 1-56280-115-5 10.95

THE FIRST TIME EVER edited by Barbara Grier & Christine Cassidy. 272 pp. Love stories by Naiad Press authors. ISBN 1-56280-086-8 14.95

MISS PETTIBONE AND MISS McGRAW by Brenda Weathers. 208 pp. A charming ghostly love story. ISBN 1-56280-151-1 10.95

CHANGES by Jackie Calhoun. 208 pp. Involved romance and relationships. ISBN 1-56280-083-3 10.95

FAIR PLAY by Rose Beecham. 256 pp. 3rd Amanda Valentine Mystery. ISBN 1-56280-081-7 10.95

PAYBACK by Celia Cohen. 176 pp. A gripping thriller of romance, revenge and betrayal. ISBN 1-56280-084-1 10.95

THE BEACH AFFAIR by Barbara Johnson. 224 pp. Sizzling summer romance/mystery/intrigue. ISBN 1-56280-090-6 10.95

GETTING THERE by Robbi Sommers. 192 pp. Nobody does it like Robbi! ISBN 1-56280-099-X 10.95

FINAL CUT by Lisa Haddock. 208 pp. 2nd Carmen Ramirez Mystery. ISBN 1-56280-088-4 10.95

FLASHPOINT by Katherine V. Forrest. 256 pp. A Lesbian blockbuster! ISBN 1-56280-079-5 10.95

CLAIRE OF THE MOON by Nicole Conn. Audio Book —Read by Marianne Hyatt. ISBN 1-56280-113-9 16.95

FOR LOVE AND FOR LIFE: INTIMATE PORTRAITS OF LESBIAN COUPLES by Susan Johnson. 224 pp. ISBN 1-56280-091-4 14.95

DEVOTION by Mindy Kaplan. 192 pp. See the movie — read the book! ISBN 1-56280-093-0 10.95

SOMEONE TO WATCH by Jaye Maiman. 272 pp. 4th Robin Miller Mystery. ISBN 1-56280-095-7 10.95

GREENER THAN GRASS by Jennifer Fulton. 208 pp. A young woman — a stranger in her bed. ISBN 1-56280-092-2 10.95

TRAVELS WITH DIANA HUNTER by Regine Sands. Erotic lesbian romp. Audio Book (2 cassettes) ISBN 1-56280-107-4 16.95

CABIN FEVER by Carol Schmidt. 256 pp. Sizzling suspense and passion. ISBN 1-56280-089-1 10.95

THERE WILL BE NO GOODBYES by Laura DeHart Young. 192 pp. Romantic love, strength, and friendship. ISBN 1-56280-103-1 10.95

FAULTLINE by Sheila Ortiz Taylor. 144 pp. Joyous comic lesbian novel. ISBN 1-56280-108-2 9.95

OPEN HOUSE by Pat Welch. 176 pp. 4th Helen Black Mystery. ISBN 1-56280-102-3 10.95

ONCE MORE WITH FEELING by Peggy J. Herring. 240 pp. Lighthearted, loving romantic adventure. ISBN 1-56280-089-2   10.95

FOREVER by Evelyn Kennedy. 224 pp. Passionate romance — love overcoming all obstacles. ISBN 1-56280-094-9   10.95

WHISPERS by Kris Bruyer. 176 pp. Romantic ghost story ISBN 1-56280-082-5   10.95

NIGHT SONGS by Penny Mickelbury. 224 pp. 2nd Gianna Maglione Mystery. ISBN 1-56280-097-3   10.95

GETTING TO THE POINT by Teresa Stores. 256 pp. Classic southern Lesbian novel. ISBN 1-56280-100-7   10.95

PAINTED MOON by Karin Kallmaker. 224 pp. Delicious Kallmaker romance. ISBN 1-56280-075-2   10.95

THE MYSTERIOUS NAIAD edited by Katherine V. Forrest & Barbara Grier. 320 pp. Love stories by Naiad Press authors. ISBN 1-56280-074-4   14.95

DAUGHTERS OF A CORAL DAWN by Katherine V. Forrest. 240 pp. Tenth Anniversay Edition. ISBN 1-56280-104-X   10.95

BODY GUARD by Claire McNab. 208 pp. 6th Carol Ashton Mystery. ISBN 1-56280-073-6   10.95

CACTUS LOVE by Lee Lynch. 192 pp. Stories by the beloved storyteller. ISBN 1-56280-071-X   9.95

SECOND GUESS by Rose Beecham. 216 pp. 2nd Amanda Valentine Mystery. ISBN 1-56280-069-8   9.95

A RAGE OF MAIDENS by Lauren Wright Douglas. 240 pp. 6th Caitlin Reece Mystery. ISBN 1-56280-068-X   10.95

TRIPLE EXPOSURE by Jackie Calhoun. 224 pp. Romantic drama involving many characters. ISBN 1-56280-067-1   10.95

UP, UP AND AWAY by Catherine Ennis. 192 pp. Delightful romance. ISBN 1-56280-065-5   9.95

PERSONAL ADS by Robbi Sommers. 176 pp. Sizzling short stories. ISBN 1-56280-059-0   10.95

CROSSWORDS by Penny Sumner. 256 pp. 2nd Victoria Cross Mystery. ISBN 1-56280-064-7   9.95

SWEET CHERRY WINE by Carol Schmidt. 224 pp. A novel of suspense. ISBN 1-56280-063-9   9.95

These are just a few of the many Naiad Press titles — we are the oldest and largest lesbian/feminist publishing company in the world. We also offer an enormous selection of lesbian video products. Please request a complete catalog. We offer personal service; we encourage and welcome direct mail orders from individuals who have limited access to bookstores carrying our publications.